VeriTales: Ring of Truth

Ring
of
Truth

Short Stories for the Evolving Spirit

Edited by Helen Wirth

Illustrated by Gail Tomura

Fall Creek Press
Fall Creek, Oregon

The short stories included in this anthology are works of fiction. Any resemblance to places, events, or persons, living or dead, is entirely coincidental.

VeriTales, the name and logo, is a trademark of:

Fall Creek Press
Post Office Box 1127
Fall Creek, Oregon 97438

Library of Congress Cataloging-in-Publication Data

VeriTales : Ring of Truth : short stories for the evolving spirit / edited by Helen Wirth ; illustrated by Gail Tomura.
    Contents: Josie / by John Vorhaus - - The painting / by Ron Suppa - - The cigarette / by Janet Howey - - Laundry Larry / by Judy Bell Carlton - - Poor devil / by David Eli Shapiro - - Requiem / by Sharlie West - - Original sin / by William Luvaas - - A secret place / by Beverly Sheresh - - Return to sender / by Terry Wolverton - - Tide pools / by Briget Laskowski - - A Lycurgus Christmas cantata / by Robert Dodge.
    ISBN 0-9632374-1-1 (pbk.) : $14.95
    1. Short Stories, American. 2. Spiritual Life- -Fiction.
I. Wirth, Helen, 1931-   . II. Title: VeriTales. III. Title: VeriTales: Ring of Truth.
PS648.S5V47 1993
813' .0108–dc20   92-45252
                                               CIP

Printed in the United States of America

Text and cover printed on recycled, acid-free paper

TABLE OF CONTENTS

A compelling romantic attraction—physical?
spiritual? Where did it begin? And where will it
end? What have we learned in a past we do not
even remember? And what difference can it
make today?

He was only twelve, his mother lay dying in the
hospital, and here he was, sharing a home with
a Bohemian aunt whose unconventional ways
left his head spinning. Words he had never
heard spoken, thoughts he would have denied
ever thinking, and an act beyond his
comprehension. The turbulence of growing up
when death comes too young.

How comfortable, and how limiting, the love of
one's childhood, which speaks in a language
both familiar and assured. How disquieting,
and how freeing, the challenge of love from a
different source.

Dexter Spivaks was such a nerd. What a relief, to
put him out of her mind and her life, once . . .
and for all? How casually, and how powerfully,
do we impact the lives of those whose paths
"unimportantly" cross our own.

His orders were to kill, and he had killed. And
the killing had returned to haunt his days, and
his dreams. The doctors could help, a little. But
only a powerful yet simple force could ever truly
break through his darkness.

JOSIE

A Veri-tale by John Vorhaus

In an infinite universe, anything is possible.

This is hell, thought Jstone Briggs as she sat jammed in the back of a Plymouth Horizon, staring out at the white-hot desert hurtling by. The cheap vinyl seats suffocated her legs, sweat-welding her thighs to her black polyester pants. Beside her sat Myung, a Vietnamese blackjack dealer, who clipped the consonants off her limited English vocabulary, so that "Have a nice day" came out, "Ha' a ni' day." Myung said "Ha' a ni' day" almost every day, but Jstone Briggs was not having a nice day.

Jstone Briggs was a day shift poker dealer at the Pyramid Casino in Copper Mine, down by the state line. She hated working in Copper Mine, but the money was better than in Cimarron, and Jstone needed good money just now. Back around Christmas her jerk of an ex-husband had drained their joint bank account and maxed out their plastic, then hit the road and left her holding the bills.

So six days a week she car-pooled down from Cimarron, an hour in hell each way, crammed in the back of this rank, cranky Plymouth Horizon next to Myung, the Vietnamese blackjack dealer. Up front, Elaine and Patti gabbed about which floorman they thought was cute and who was doing what to whom on their favorite soap operas, which they videotaped religiously. Thank heaven for videotape; they'd sooner miss work than miss a single gripping episode. The car's air conditioning had gone south during the first hot days of May, and now it was all Jstone could do to keep from passing out. Far in the distance a dust devil swirled across a dry lake bed. *This really is hell,* thought Jstone, sweat dripping into her eyes, *and I'm serving a life sentence.*

A silver Lincoln Continental swept by, all elegant lines, and grace, and power, and cobalt blue tinted windows. The driver, a small man, animated with high energy, tapped his hands on the steering wheel and sang along to some unheard song. Looking over at

Jstone, he shot her a wink and a grin. Then he was past, speeding off down the road toward Copper Mine, which loomed now in the distance like a chrome steel mirage, laid out dead on the desert floor. Jstone's eyes rolled up and she fled from the heat to a cool, dark corner of her mind. . . .

Jstone Briggs had acquired her odd first name from her father, J. Stone Whitman, a Tulsa oil rigger who never quite forgave her for not being a boy. She grew up with deft, clever fingers, an ironic eye, and an unforced sense of humor. She had a gift for drawing cartoons, but her father soon bullied the art out of her, leaving Jstone a sullen, hard-eyed teenager, who called herself Josie and vowed to leave home the first chance she got.

She met Bobby Briggs in a cowboy bar, where he charmed her with his silver dollar smile and his grand plans for moving to Cimarron and taking sin city by stealth. He seemed to be the Gypsy Davy, an outlaw gambler who'd help her punish her father for being so mean. She packed a bag one midnight and left without saying good-bye.

They were married before she knew his last name, and she spent the next six years feeding his jones for making eight the hard way. She finally kicked him out, but he picked her clean before he left.

11

Now she was picking up the pieces, burning up her life on the highway between Cimarron and Copper Mine. But always her eyes looked west, to the California coast, where the air blew in cool off the ocean. In her mind's eye Josie saw a sunlit studio and a drawing table, where cartoons took life beneath her fervent pen. But that was only a dream; and dreams, Josie knew, were just something you had when you'd had too much to drink, or when the rhythm of a Plymouth's cheap shock absorbers lulled you into blissful, merciful sleep. . . .

"Josie?" Patti's gentle hand shook her awake. "Josie, honey, wake up. We're there." Jstone opened her eyes and hauled herself out of the car, her muscles aching with cramped protest. Head bowed by the heat, she stumbled up to the smoked glass doors of the Pyramid Casino.

The Pyramid had a New Age theme, and teased people with the fantasy that their own strong psychic energy could control the roll of the dice or the turn of a card or the drop of a slot machine's reels. Everywhere you turned you saw huge glittering crystals and giant-sized Tarot cards and other totems of powerful magic. Josie smiled wryly at the decor. She knew from grim personal experience that there was no magic here.

Jstone was about halfway through her shift, dealing low-limit seven-card stud, when an odd, small man sat down directly opposite her in seat number four. He wasn't short so much as compact, as if he'd been built to seven/eighths scale. Although he was almost completely bald, his face was smooth and unlined, so that he seemed simultaneously old and young. He looked at Jstone and shot her a wink and a smile. Something about the gesture registered with her, but before she could follow the thought, he was reading her name tag aloud. "'Josie?'" he said. "That's not your real name, is it?" Somehow he managed to sound both challenging and disarming.

"No," she answered, "it's Jstone, but people find that hard to pronounce."

"I see," said the man. "My name is Phil. Phil Cupid. People don't generally find that hard to pronounce." She wondered if he meant that as a joke, but his open, expressive face suggested otherwise. It was just a statement of fact.

About ten minutes into his play he said quietly, "Josie, I'd like a seven just now. Could you please concentrate on dealing me a seven?"

Briefly, almost involuntarily, she pictured a seven in her head. A seven hit the felt. Phil didn't seem surprised. He laid down a straight to the eight, and collected a large pot. "Thank you," he said. Though his words seemed sincere, he didn't tip her and Josie inwardly bristled. Didn't this guy know you're supposed to tip? Judging from his blank expression, no.

Ten minutes later Josie went on break, then returned to deal to the other two games going in the Pyramid's card room. When she returned to Phil's table, he didn't ask her to think of any cards; nor did he tip her when he won. The other players took notice. Thatcher, an obscene chain-smoker, short on tact, snorted at last and said, "Hey, big shot, girl's gotta eat, you know."

"Excuse me?" asked Phil, bemused, yet placid.

"You're supposed to toke a pretty dealer when you win a hand, that's all."

"I see," Phil answered. He didn't say anything more.

Three hands later Phil fixed his gaze on Josie and said, "I think I need a jack now. Please think of a jack, Jstone." Josie thought, *Damned if I'm going to think of a jack for you, Mr. High Roller.* Which thought, of course, only brought a jack to mind.

She gasped just a little when she dealt the jack of diamonds into Phil's hand. Phil laid down trip jacks and took the pot. Again he thanked her modestly and genuinely. Again he didn't tip.

Shortly before Josie's shift ended, Phil was working on a club flush when he spoke to her one last time. "Any club will do, Josie," he said, "but I really want the king. Would you please think of the king of clubs? Hmm?"

She tried not to think of the king of clubs, but there it was, filling his hand, completing his royal flush. Josie looked around nervously, wondering if anyone thought she was in cahoots with this creep. A few minutes later she went off shift, glad to leave the weirdness behind.

Josie was sitting at a video poker machine, working a crossword puzzle, as she waited for Elaine and Patti and Myung, and the long ride home in the heat. Sensing motion nearby, she looked up to see Phil standing over her. "You deal nicely," he said. "May I sit down?" Not waiting for an answer, he sat. "I didn't tip you," he said.

"Intuitive grasp of the obvious there, bright boy," she growled.

"Would you like to know why?"

"Would you like to tell me?"

He smiled. "Good answer. Yes, I'd like to tell you. I didn't tip you because I have something much more valuable to give you."

"Yeah? What's that?"

"A ride home."

"You've got some juice, fella. First you make me look like I'm feeding you cards, then you stiff me, and *then* you try and pick me up?"

"You don't want a ride?"

"Buzz off."

He fixed her with his gaze. Suddenly, she remembered him from the car, that silver Lincoln Continental. Or not remembered exactly; more like she saw a picture of herself, riding back up to Cimarron in that Lincoln, with the air conditioner going full blast in her face. *Why not?* she thought. *Always take cookies when cookies are passed.*

At last, she said, "I live up in Cimarron, you know."

"Of course," he answered. "Who'd live in Copper Mine?"

"If I let you drive me home, will you tell me how you did that stunt with the cards?"

"Of course. Why else would I want to drive you home?"

So Josie found herself sinking in butter-soft leather seats, chill air drying the sweat from her shirt, as the desert fled by in the twilight. She had to admit, it looked better through the cold, closed windows of a Lincoln Continental. Almost beautiful. Almost.

"So," said Phil at last, "how is your art coming?"

She shot him a quick glance. "What makes you think I'm an artist?"

"Educated guess," he said. "A poker player has to be perceptive." She fleetingly imagined him skulking around her house, prying into her life. He laughed. "No, Josie, I don't peek in windows."

"Look," said Josie, rattled, "maybe you'd better let me out here."

Phil scanned the horizon. Nothing but dust and basalt as far as the eye could see. "Here?"

"Well, maybe not here. But just can the fantasy, huh?"

"Very well, no fantasy. How about science fiction? Astronomers now tell us that ninety per cent of the universe is comprised of dark matter which we don't really understand at all. Think of it, Josie: the whole history of human knowledge behind us, and the best we can muster is ten per cent of total understanding. No wonder life is such a mystery."

"Yeah, well, okay, you like mysteries so much, why don't you tell me how you froze my deck? God knows what my floorman thought. A dealer's reputation is gold, you know."

"And I have no thought to tarnish that precious gem, Josie. It just so happens that you can call up any card you picture in your mind."

"That's impossible."

"My dear, in an infinite universe, anything is possible."

"So why'd I never do it before?"

"Maybe you never had the proper . . . focus. Maybe with the right kind of help you could do it all the time."

Josie froze. "What are you saying, exactly?"

"What I am saying, *exactly*," he answered in a mocking tone, "is that you should consider *playing* cards instead of dealing them. Assuming you still want your house by the sea, that is."

"Look, just stop, okay? I don't know what your game is, but find another playmate."

Phil ignored her protest. "You'll want proof, I imagine. There's a beer truck about a mile down the road, Josie. It's heading this way. What brand of beer is it hauling?"

"How should I . . ."

"*Think* about it."

So Josie thought about it. She thought of the most obscure label she could name, *Tulsa Town*, the kind of beer her father used to drink.

"He beat you, didn't he?"

"*What?*"

"Hush. Here comes your truck."

A lumbering eighteen-wheeler crested a hill in the distance. Josie watched the truck approach, quite certain that it carried Bud, or Miller, or probably not even beer at all, and that she could soon put this whole nonsense to rest.

The truck closed. It passed. *Tulsa Town.*

"Jesus!" Josie looked over at Phil, wide- eyed. "What *are* you?" she whispered.

"I'm the delivery man," he said. "I deliver people's dreams."

They still talk about the lucky streak that Jstone Briggs enjoyed in Cimarron that summer. She started with low-limit games, but quickly moved up, as her bankroll swelled. Soon she was sitting in on—and busting—the biggest games in town. And everywhere she went, she had this weird homunculus sidekick, riding the rail behind her.

Sometimes, when she needed a case card or a difficult inside catch, they'd both become lost in thought—communing, it seemed, with some higher power. Other players learned to fear those moments, for sure as the house takes its rake, when Josie and Phil screwed down their eyes, the card Josie needed was about to hit the felt. When it did, she would always smile and say, "Thus does a blind pig find an acorn in the snow." And she'd reach behind her and give Phil's hand a squeeze.

There was nothing like romance between them, only the closeness wrought of partnership, and long hours spent together. Josie appreciated what Phil was doing for her, but every now and then she'd catch him looking at her, studying her, sizing her up, almost. In her heart of hearts he kind of gave her the creeps. She was careful to guard those thoughts, but she wondered if it made any difference. He seemed to know everything about her anyhow.

One night in early autumn, at the Fort Cimarron Hotel and Casino, she went head-to-head with

Alabama Jack Hazzard, arguably the finest no-limit hold 'em player alive. She cleaned him out in just over two hours. He tipped his hat as he left, and Josie let out a whoop of triumph. In that moment, in that single perfect moment, there was no past or future for her, no cruel father, no shiftless ex-husband, but also no home on the California coast. She suddenly realized she was exactly where she wanted to be. And she was happy.

Later, long after midnight, she and Phil sat at the bar of the Cowboy Lip Saloon, adjacent to the big pits, filled with table games and squawky late night action. Al, the bartender, brought them fresh drinks: spring water for Josie, a tequila braindeath for Phil.

"Well, my dear Josie," said Phil, "by my math, you now have over two hundred thousand dollars, cash."

"Yeah, not bad for a Tulsa girl, huh?"

"Not bad at all. And now I imagine you're about ready to leave Cimarron and go set up shop on the coast."

"What are you, high? I've only just started to milk these bozos."

"I see. But what about your house and your ocean view? What about your art?"

"Forget that, I'm doing too well to quit."

"Hmm. This disturbs me, Jstone. I hadn't imagined squandering both our talents on the mere accumulation of wealth."

"Hang on, pal. You're not thinking of pulling the plug, are you? I thought you wanted to help make my dream come true."

"Was this your dream?"

"Okay, so it's a different dream."

"I was not aware," he said slowly, "that dreams could change so fast."

"Well, they can. Look at me, Phil. I'm no cartoonist. I've never sold a single drawing. But I'm a poker player now, and a damn good one. If it ain't broke, don't fix it, huh?"

Phil sighed. "I see. In that case," he said, standing, "I believe our partnership is at an end."

"What? You can't go. I need you."

"Well, while it's nice to be needed, I'm afraid I have no choice. You see, according to my timetable, you were supposed to be in California by now. Since you're not there yet, I can only guess that you will never get there. It would be pointless for me to remain."

"But what about the money?"

"Money, my dear, is only a means to an end. I had hoped to help you see that."

"You double-crosser! You take me halfway up the mountain, and then you *leave* me there? How dare you? I trusted you!"

"And I you."

"Well, fine. Leave if you want to, you little creep! I don't need you anyhow. My game's not all luck, you know. I can win on my own, without any help from you." Josie's voice rose to a defiant high pitch. "It's possible. You said it yourself: in an infinite universe, anything is possible."

"And so it is, my dear. And so it certainly is." Phil Cupid walked away. Josie hurled a bottle at him as he left.

It's sad what happened next. Without Phil's magic touch—or without the confidence that his presence bred—Josie went on tilt, a fabulous, mind-boggling skid, that didn't end until she had lost back every penny she had won that summer. To say that she couldn't afford the buy-in to a freeroll was barely overstating the case.

By the time she hit bottom, Josie was living on the street, wandering around in a self-made maze, her mind a riot of high walls surrounding a thicket of regret. She wished she could go back in time, leave the game a winner, and follow her old dream to that house on the California coast. But Josie knew—perhaps better than anyone—that dreams are just something people have when they've had too much to drink. She felt like she'd been drunk all year. It was time to sober up.

And so it was the following May that Josie found herself once more riding down to Copper Mine, working as a change runner at the Pyramid Casino, working her way back from a hell of her own making. She no longer minded the drive. Patti's ratty Plymouth Horizon didn't seem hateful now. It was soothing, somehow, like an old, familiar friend with whom she had long lost touch.

Slowly, painstakingly, Jstone Briggs was starting to rebuild her life. She even placed a couple of cartoons in the Pyramid Casino's house newsletter. One sketch showed half-a-dozen skeletons sitting around a poker table. The caption read, "One more hand."

The day after that drawing appeared, an overstuffed manila envelope arrived, addressed to her at the Pyramid Casino. When Josie opened it, she discovered inside ten thousand dollars in crisp one hundred dollar bills—and a note.

The note read: *To Josie, who rediscovered her dream. Here's your tip at last.*

Josie quit her job on the spot. She hitchhiked up to Cimarron, went straight to the airport, and bought a ticket for the next flight to the California coast. She practically danced through the terminal, whistling all the way to the plane.

Someone watched her board that plane, a tidy little man who hid himself behind a newspaper in an airport bar. He watched her go, and he shot her a wink and a nod which she didn't even see. Then the little man got up and walked away, past a row of slot machines, where a newlywed couple plunked dollars into a one-armed bandit. "I don't know why we're playing this darned thing," said the husband. "It's impossible to win."

In an infinite universe, thought Phil Cupid, *anything is possible.*

He left the airport with the sound of a slot machine jackpot and the newlyweds' delighted squeals still ringing in his ears.

The Painting

A Veri-tale by Ron Suppa

I was only nineteen when I climbed a whole mountainside in the rain for you. The ups have been harder since then, and last night, wondering if I'd slipped all the way down this time, I thought of us that summer in Bali, where you said we had found our Eden.

On a rented motorcycle we had left Sanur Beach, the "inter-continental crowd" you called them, for the sunset side of the island, where no house was higher than a coconut tree and the coastline lay deserted save for a few children picking for shells in the shallow tide. The Balinese are a religious people, frightened of the sea, believing that God lives high in the mountains and only evil dwells beneath the surface of the ocean. Wary of lingering too long with the devil, they never swim in the miles of clear blue waters and rarely even fish from a sea teeming with food.

From the first light of dawn we rode past lush hillsides, rich with tropical plants of red and gold and violet and grass greener than any green we'd ever seen before. We rested under an enormous knotted banyan tree to shade us from the sun. It was twelve hours' ride to Kuta Beach, past a world that time had left untouched: villages entered through six-foot-high mazes of mud and clay, built to confuse the evil spirits; giant ferns and wildflowers, cascading from red lava cliffs; rice farmers, wearing yellow hats like saucers to shield them from the sun, working fields carved from hillsides in lush green steps. Heaven, to the Balinese, is exactly like Bali.

By early afternoon your head had carved its own place snug between my shoulder blades. Your arms seemed attached to my waist. When the road gave out, it left us sputtering over a blanket of ancient royal graves, half-hidden by the growth in the coffee fields. We picnicked on one. We even detoured three hours to climb to the volcano lakes, where we tried to bathe, but the water was freezing (you stripped bare; I was too shy, even if only the mountain gods were watching.)

Throughout the countryside we encountered weavers and woodcarvers and silversmiths, and women in brightly colored batiks, carrying groceries on their heads and walking pet pigs on leashes of rope and leather. And everywhere, children, throngs and throngs of children, in teeshirts and shorts and sandals, eating curries wrapped in palm leaves, and chewing betel nuts, and flirting with the young girls in yellow cotton dresses behind the food stands that lined every road.

We learned that when a young woman came of marrying age she was made to work the stands, so that she might be seen by the widest possible choice of men. When she caught the fancy of a desirable partner, he bought lunch from her—every day—until she showed her assent to marry by charging him less than the going rate. That night, as her parents pretended to sleep, he would kidnap her from her home and carry her away for his bride.

The important things were simple on Bali, but ceremony and custom were always observed. Like finding that everyone we met seemed to have the same name. At a hostel on the sunrise side, where we paid forty cents for two soft cots and a breakfast of tea and cakes, a one-eyed Dutchman (who we thought was blind) told us that all Balinese are given one of four names at birth: Wayen for the first born, Made for the next, then Noyman and Ketut, and back to Wayen for a fifth child, as the names rotate round again. A teen-age girl named Noyman, who spoke pidgin English, became our guide in Legion for a nickel. I think you may have been a bit jealous, because you kept separating her hand from mine when she would lead us along the way. I never told you that I had given her a quarter because I was sure you had hurt her feelings.

It was past midnight, with no moon to give us light, as we threaded our way through the elephant grass and coconut trees to a secluded cove where we hoped to spend the night. The wind was coming hard off the shore and we made a lean-to out of a partly burnt wooden platform and some bamboo poles we found near the treeline. To your horror we later discovered that they were left over from a ceremonial burning of corpses a night earlier; death, like life, is a religious event for the Balinese.

Do you remember the ritual burial we saw in the village before we left? The rhythmic beating of the gamelan echoed through us like bad jazz; you feared it was never going to end. The natives had been up since dawn, prancing about in elegant white silk and golden headdresses, and celebrating with mask dances and tables full of fruit and meats and breads—one last supper to share with the deceased. Then the body was lifted high in the air and spun round and round to confuse the soul, so it wouldn't wander back some stormy night and scare the hair off their children's heads.

Actually, except for certain high priests privileged not to reside even a day below the topsoil, most Balinese must endure a temporary grave before cremation, since the latter is a costly affair often shared by more than one aggrieved family. A platform is constructed under a wooden tower, complete with mirrored roofs and jewels and rainbowed fabrics, and held up by bamboo poles covered in ornamental paper. It is believed that the platform holds the dead between earth and heaven. Only when the body is destroyed and the ashes purified by tossing them into the sea is the soul free to enter heaven and be reborn, fresh and clean, to a better world.

The whole ritual was fascinating to me—maybe that's why I remember it all so well—but I know it only gave you the creeps. You didn't sleep much that night and insisted on sharing a sleeping bag despite the heat.

Then, very seriously and deliberately, you married our body parts to one another, your left leg to my right, your right to my left, belly to belly, lips to lips, each coupling being taken for better or for worse, for richer or for poorer, till death do us part. You said that we could never separate the parts again for longer than a day. I fell sound asleep while you were still talking. These days I suffer from insomnia most every night.

When we awoke in the morning to waves four feet from our four feet, we found that the young girl, Noyman, had left a basket lid in front of our lean-to, full with rice, fruit, red leaves, yellow flower petals, and the quarter I had given her the day before. She had made the offering on our behalf, so the Gods would spare us harm.

It was late the next afternoon, while looking for a sarong for you, that we saw the painting on the wall of the tailor shop. Fully six feet by five, in shades of blue and green and pale yellow ocher, it depicted an old Balinese legend which the tailor's wife explained to us in flawless French. It seems that long ago the Prince had sent his favorite messenger to a far off village to fetch a chosen princess for his bride. Do you remember the painting now? In it, the messenger has returned and sits on horseback near the mounted princess and her entourage, their faces turned away from the Prince in pain and shame. It is apparent to the Prince that he has been betrayed, however unintended the betrayal; the princess and the messenger have fallen in love.

Even the cockatoos and parrots and marsupials in the trees and the giant lizards on the forest floor bore pained expressions, as did you and I when we learned that the painting wasn't for sale. You had already determined it to be the one gift you wanted to bring back from the islands. The old lady liked you a lot and managed to tell us where we could locate the artist, but since we were leaving the next day, we had to find her that very night.

The rainy season was supposed to end in April, and it being August, the clouds had no business dripping over us all day and then, as we climbed a steep mountainside toward the painter's village, dumping their load by the gallons, until I was forced to plod behind you to hold you up straight in the mud. By sundown we were getting nowhere fast and your tears were mixing with the rain (you upset easily when you were frustrated), so I left you in a warm and cozy hut with a bevy of children hypnotized by your long, blond hair and you by their laughter.

It was cold and wet and lonely, and I more than a little scared going on up that mountain without you, and how I found that lady I'll never really know, but a wave here and a question there kept me pointed in the right direction. And when I entered the portal of her lair, thatched and inviting as a robin's nest—the single entrance had no door—I knew I had arrived.

It was the eclectic abode of an artist. Amidst carvings and paintings and pots and clothes in disarray, silver hair to her knees and tied in knots along her back, she sat calmly, as if she had known me all my life, and gave me mint tea and pork with a spicy nut dressing and an assortment of fruits and a coconut with soft insides. Mostly, she understood why I was there. From the paintings leaning against her wall I described the painting I had seen and she nodded and smiled and said, I thought, two weeks.

This was not good news, but I had certainly not come all that way for nothing and I could just picture your face if I gave up on your prize this close to the finish line. So I showed her what money I had and she picked and chose among the bills and coins, and she wasn't all that cheap. Over fifty dollars, U.S., I'd figure now, though then it seemed she just was taking whatever wasn't sticking to my palm. The first pangs of Yankee doubt had planted seed. Was I being taken for the proverbial long ride, I thought, as I waved goodbye with empty pockets?

By the time I made my way down to you, darkness had long since settled in, and I do believe you were angry and ready for a row. But seeing me dragging my body along, obviously cold and tired and wet, you made one of the wise decisions of your young life and let it pass, saying how we'd probably find the painting waiting for us when we reached the States. I think you knew that I knew that you doubted it too, but you acted excited anyway, and that made me feel much better.

Well, we made it back to the sunrise side the next day and were home in San Francisco before the fall, and that winter we'd broken up and by spring you had left for New York. I heard that a year later you were engaged and it's been fifteen now since I saw you then. We never really brought it up again, the painting never having come and all, but I think we both felt a little cheated and naive and made a mental note not to trust so easily again and to pull the shell around us a little tighter. It was not a lesson you should have learned.

You see, almost fourteen months after you left, twenty since I'd shared some tea with an artist in Bali, the post office sent me notice that they were holding, wrapped in a long white sheet that might have once warmed the head of some visiting Arab sheik, a very long and hollow tube with postage due. If you have ever seen the sunset bouncing off the Colosseum in Rome, or a freshly snow-kissed mountain morning in Courchevel, you may have felt as newly-born as I, sitting in an apartment in postal zone 94123, having connected with a little gentlewoman named Made, living somewhere in the hills of Bali.

Last night I turned thirty-four. With a bottle for one I celebrated, staring at that perfect canvas hanging on a wall. I've had it moved and hung a dozen times over the years, hoping someday along the way to be able to give you back your souvenir, and maybe get a hug from you. Sometimes I have the sense of you here, but not the movement of the air by the sheer weight of your body, not the smell of your skin nor the warmth of your smile.

Every now and then I drift off into another space and time, thinking of you, wishing I could be transported to you and see your face, that oval face shining clean, the way you've fixed your hair, how you look now. And in my dreams I step into your painting and walk through the forest toward the outstretched limbs of the banyan tree, where everything is cool and clean smelling and possible, as the Balinese think it possible to watch a rock grow or drink tea from an empty cup.

But last night I took the painting down and put it away, this time for the last time. A temporary burial before the cremation. Dust to dust and ashes to the purifying sea. For I was only nineteen, after all, when I climbed a whole mountainside in the pouring rain in Bali just to find you a picture that you loved. And I believed in that old lady as I believe in you still, but sometimes, my love, the waiting is too long.

THE CIGARETTE

A Veri-tale by Janet Howey

I was afraid to go outside yet, because the day was so uncomfortably lovely. Mid-September, and the air and sun both soft, the petunias and roses and lobelia blooming big and late and everywhere, sitting so still in delicious laziness. The self-confidence of the splendor frightened me, and I wanted to stay safe from that skin-peeling beauty while I waited for *it* to happen.

I'd been waiting for *it* to happen sincesome time Thursday night. I couldn't find anything on TV, and instead of picking up a book or calling a friend, I lay on the couch, pressing the remote control like a trigger on a gun, shooting the TV over and over. But nothing there would satisfy me, and I knew that TV wasn't *it*.

I got into bed, but sleep made only a grudging visit. I rose, late and irritable, exhausted with frustration that *it* hadn't happened, not even in my dreams.

So Friday began. I don't see therapy clients on Friday. That's my day to finish up on paperwork at home. But when I picked up the insurance forms and tried to fill in the "diagnosis" and "prognosis," I felt only the absurdity of describing people that way, and was furious that in order to get paid, I had to participate in such silliness.

In ten minutes I closed the desk and called my answering service. Maybe this would be *it*. A telephone call. From an old boyfriend maybe. The one who hurt me in college twenty years ago, calling to say he's sorry. Or maybe the man who turned in the winning lottery ticket yesterday decided I was more deserving. He'd call to say he'd like to split the winnings, and then I'd have to think about so many new things and reorganize my life. Or my doctor might call to say she'd just discovered some of my old test results, lost in a file, and I'd better come in right away. I'd have to face a terrible disease and that would be *it*.

But when I called the service, they said there'd been only two calls since I checked the night before, both from clients needing to reschedule. My voice cracked as I thanked the operator. I hung up and decided to do some errands.

On my way to the pet store I passed La Casa Rosa, the shop that sells Mexican and South American clothes. That's me. An aging hippie, decked out in bright clothes made in foreign countries. I wouldn't have stopped, but an old Honda Civic pulled out, leaving a parking space right in front of the store. I took that as a sign that this might be *it*. Inside the store I quickly sorted through the racks. Not my color, not my size, too much of what I already have, outrageously expensive. The place disgusted me and I was out in six minutes.

At the pet store the clerk said he had to check in the back, since I wanted a whole case of cat food. Suddenly, I feared that would take too long, that *it* might happen while I was waiting. Or that I would wait and wait, and *it* wouldn't happen. I bought one can of food—that would last a day—and hurried home to confront the mailbox.

By now I was losing hope. Still, I couldn't ignore the possibilities: a magazine, soliciting my writing; an invitation to speak; some sort of confirmation that I not only existed, but existed importantly.

The pile of mail was thin. Two clothing catalogs, three bills, an announcement about a neighborhood meeting. My insides disappeared. Empty of ballast, I lay down on my bed, fully clothed, and wrapped myself tight in my quilt. It was one in the afternoon. I was not sleepy. Sleep was not *it*. I stared at the ceiling for two hours, holding my body very still. Unexposed. Invisible.

I didn't call anyone over the weekend, though I kept checking with the service to see if there had been any messages from *it*, or explaining *it*, or even referring to *it*. There were none. I let the messages from my friends pile up. I did not want to fill the air with empty sounds, or the sounds of my own voice, talking about *it* as if I knew what *it* was, as if *it* had touched me, as if I no longer despaired of ever knowing *it*.

Sunday night was both the easiest and the most difficult, because I had given up hope. All I had left was an aimless, muted anger that rested in a hard ball behind my eyes as I waited for numbing sleep.

I dreaded this morning, Monday, this too-pretty morning, because I had three clients today. I would have to rise before my agitation became clearly formed, recognizable. As each of my clients sat in my office, I would have to try to care about their world, when without *it,* what world could possibly matter?

I dressed for the day, fearing what would happen if my despair became larger than my body and spilled out on a downtown street. As I fumbled through my dresser drawer, vaguely searching for my Indian bead necklace, my thoughts were suddenly interrupted. There, hidden behind my sewing kit, dusty but only half-crushed, lay a lone cigarette.

For the first time since Thursday my eyes focused clearly. My immediate thought was, "No way. I don't smoke." For I had put out my last cigarette three months earlier. But then came the belligerent response, "I'm grown up. I can smoke if I want to."

Gently, almost lovingly, I lifted the cigarette out of the drawer. I dusted it, rolled it lightly between my palms, packed it, smelled it, smiled. My mind was still, my stomach miraculously quiet. "This little cigarette," I thought. "This sweet little cigarette. I think this may be *it.*" Perfect. I wouldn't have to buy a pack. I wouldn't have to become a Smoker. Just one cigarette to fill up the holes in me. Just for today.

Savoring my salvation, I rather easily decided not to smoke right away. I could wait one more hour, until I got to the office. I would smoke the cigarette there, giving myself plenty of time to feel every drag, before my first client arrived. And when Elizabeth Matthews came in for her nine o'clock appointment, I would be able to pay attention. I would be interested in what she had to say. I might even guide her through some difficulty. I might make a difference.

The timing, too, was perfect. Mary Beth, the other therapist in the suite, didn't see her first client until noon on Mondays. I had sublet the space from her right after I quit smoking. In my newly-converted zeal I had assured her I would have no problem with her no-smoking policy. After I finished smoking my one cigarette today, I would open the window and use breath freshener. By noon she would never suspect.

With the cigarette and matches in my pocket, the ash tray and breath mints in my purse, I left my house this morning, holding September's beauty at bay. The animated chatter of the Chinese woman to her bored teen-age daughter on the bus, the city skyline, the smell of coffee on Pioneer Square, all these I also held at bay. But I knew they were there. I was saving them. *It* was going to happen soon, and after *it* happened, the curtain that separated me from my life would fall away.

When I reached the office, I took off my jacket slowly and hung it precisely on its hanger. I cleared my desk of papers, wound the clock that faithfully terminates each appointment, arranged myself comfortably in my chair, took a deep breath, and reached into my skirt pocket for the cigarette. I placed the filter between my lips and sighed into delicious familiarity. Finally, I lit the match, held it to the tip of the cigarette, and inhaled.

Everything stopped. Fear, anger, restlessness, emptiness, distance. All gone in one puff. I felt no deep satisfaction. There was only relief, the end of wanting. But that was enough.

I took another drag. Dry tartness clung to the roof of my mouth, a familiar, unpleasant sensation. I studied my fingernails, noted two that needed clipping, did nothing about them.

On the third drag hot, dusty, foul-smelling bitterness seared the back of my throat, bit my lungs. I erupted into a seizure. Hacking, gagging, wheezing, I dropped the cigarette into the ashtray, wrapped my bursting ribs in my arms, and doubled over. Panicky for air, I coughed and choked into exhaustion, and then filled up with sobs. Still holding my ribs, I stared at the cigarette. "Shit," I hissed. "You're not *it*."

Fear surged through me now. I felt it crawling, legs to throat. Rage roared through next, then despair. Wave after wave. My brain pounded at my skull; my face and hands were wet with tears and mucous. The ticking of the clock on the table was the only steadiness I could feel, and slowly, faithfully, its steadiness subdued me.

In the quiet of my final whimpers I heard the bell ring on the door to the outer office. I wiped the streaks of eyeliner from my face and ran a brush through my straggly hair, then slipped on my jacket to cover my wrinkled blouse and stepped out into the waiting room.

Elizabeth Matthews smiled at me. The contrast of her thick, white hair and white cotton dress against her smooth, black skin made her an arresting presence. I had forgotten how much I liked her.

"Hello, Elizabeth."

"How you doin', Marie?"

"Well, not too well, actually. I came in this morning to meet with you, but if you could come in tomorrow at nine instead, I think I could do a better job for you."

"Okay," she began. I eased gratefully into the comfort of her predictable good nature. "If you think that will give you enough time, I'll see you then. Feel better." And she was out the door.

I walked back into my office, leaving the door slightly ajar. I sat down, sighed . . . and heard the bell on the outer office ring again. The door closed. High heels tapped across the floor. Mary Beth wore high heels. My heart, finally quiet, jumped again. The door to her office opened. I reached forward, knocking my telephone to the floor, and squashed the cigarette hard into the ash tray. Leaning down for the phone, I heard the high heels again and then a tap on my door. Seeing my purse under the desk, I dropped the phone, sat up, grabbed the cigarette and ash tray, and shoved them into my bag.

The door opened wider, and there was Mary Beth. She stands six feet tall without her heels and wears her black hair pulled tight in a bun. Today, her bright blue shoes matched the solid blue of her skirt and jacket, her blue-framed designer glasses and her ceramic cobalt earrings. Her lips were unabashedly red, and right then she was the biggest person I had ever seen.

"Sorry to disturb you. Got a minute to chat?" she asked.

Mary Beth and I didn't "chat" much. I hadn't known her before I sublet the space. She did mostly couples counseling and sex therapy, which I wouldn't touch with a ten-foot pole, so we didn't have much to talk about professionally, and we definitely never discussed wardrobe.

"Sure, have a seat." I pointed to the couch where my clients sit. She sat down, but she didn't say anything.

"What's up?" I asked nervously. "You're not usually in so early on Monday."

"Oh, I have to meet with the landlord, and I have a bunch of paperwork to catch up on, so I decided to start early."

"Oh. Uh huh." Silence.

She pointed at the floor. "I thought you might want to pick that up first," she said, nodding at the telephone splayed at my feet. The handset was three feet from the machine and the cord was wrapped around the wheels of my chair, rendering it immobile.

"Oh, right, yeah. That's just what I was doing when you came in."

She nodded, and I retrieved the phone. I looked at her again. She was studying the room. "Well, I just wanted to tell you that I'm having the outer office and my office painted. You can have yours done too if you'd like. I know this is short notice, but the landlord would like to know the colors today. I have some samples for you here."

I gaped at her. "That's what you wanted to talk to me about?"

"Mm-hmm." Her eyebrows raised in mild surprise.

It was a very difficult moment for me. For just as I realized that Mary Beth had not come to chastise me about smoking, I realized something else. Somewhere, very close to me, fiber was burning. As casually as I could, I glanced over my left shoulder in the direction of the smell.

"Uh, well, I think this office looks pretty good, don't you?" Mary Beth said nothing. My eyes rested on my woven Guatemalan purse on the floor behind me. A fine plume of smoke was curling through the seam. I turned back to face Mary Beth. Now her eyes and eyebrows were moving, surveying, puzzling. Her mouth was still.

"I mean, there aren't any serious marks on the walls or anything, and I like this eggshell color just fine. So . . . no, don't worry about me. Uh . . . actually, I'm afraid I've got to get back to all this paper."

"Sure. But if you change your mind, let me know today, will you?" She got up slowly, very slowly, and walked to the door. She stood for an instant, holding the knob, and I thought I noticed, before she walked out, that her nostrils flared just faintly.

I grabbed a blanket from the couch, threw it over the smoke, and jumped wildly on the purse. Then I ran to the sink. Using my coffee cup as a fire bucket, I doused the fire three times, then fell into my chair, holding my head in my hands. A few minutes later I touched the purse. Cold and damp. I was out of danger. Out of *that* danger. I drank a cup of water, emptied my purse, and surveyed the damage. Burn holes in the purse and carpet; a smoke stain on the blanket; broken sunglasses, mirror, tampon case; charred ID; charred, water-logged dollar bills. Only the coins had survived unscathed.

I stared at the floor where the mess was displayed, and when I shook my head a muffled chuckle tumbled out. Leaving the mess untouched, I called my answering service. Gerald Ramsey, my ten o'clock, had canceled. Perfect. I picked up the phone to cancel Ginny Wester at eleven, then changed my mind. I took a deep breath, walked out the door, and tapped on Mary Beth's office.

"Come on in, Marie."

"Hi again."

"Hi. Have a seat."

"Well . . . uh . . . maybe in a minute. I actually just wanted to . . . uh . . . tell you something. . . . I mean . . . it's something I did. . . . I didn't mean to offend you. . . . I just . . ."

The bright red, precisely defined corners of Mary Beth's mouth were creeping slowly upward. "You just set your purse on fire," she said.

"Well, actually, yes." I exploded with relief. "I set my purse on fire. That's exactly what I did. I threw a lit cigarette into my purse and set it on fire." I grinned at her boldly.

A giggle bounced in her throat. "Mm-hmm. I smelled the cigarette when I first walked into your office, and I guess in the back of my mind I knew that's what the fire was all about." She laughed, holding her forehead in her hand.

"And you didn't say anything?" I sat down.

"No. I like to think I'm pretty straightforward, but I'll be damned if I know how to say, 'Excuse me, I believe that cigarette you're hiding from me has set your purse on fire.' I guess I didn't care too much about your purse, and I assumed you'd get things under control before the whole room went up in flames." She was laughing hard now, wiping her eyes with her handkerchief (blue, of course), so I laughed too. We laughed until our make-up painted us in all the wrong places and our ribs and stomachs hurt too much to laugh any more.

Finally, Mary Beth rocked back in her chair. "I smoked for twenty years," she said. "Quit three years ago . . . went through hell."

"Boy, I guess. I smoked for just ten, and this weekend was awful. Before that I thought I was doing fine."

"Yeah, it can go like that."

"It gets easier, right? Tell me it gets easier."

"Oh, sure. You get your skin back on eventually. But I was naked to the bones for a long time." She opened her little refrigerator, offered me a glass of juice, and went on with her tales. How she'd quit four times before she made it stick; how one time she got fat, and another time, impossibly manic; how her husband told her that grouchy was okay sometimes, but just plain mean was not; how she knew it was all worth it, but even now there were times at a party when she'd smell a cigarette and want to sit right down in the smoker's lap.

Her voice soothed me like a comforting dream. I sipped the pineapple juice, felt it tingle on my tongue and splash into my stomach, emptied out now from laughter and sobs. Sitting back in Mary Beth's blue armchair, inhaling clean, smokeless air, I felt that emptiness floating through me, so smooth and delicious that it filled me completely.

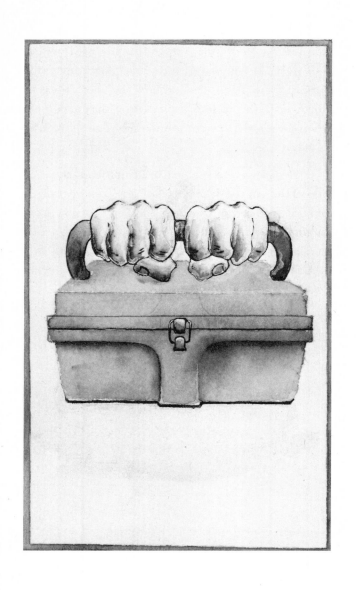

LAUNDRY LARRY

A Veri-tale by Judy Bell Carlton

Larry lumbered clumsily up the bus steps, his thick, stubby fingers clutching his bus pass. He nodded to the driver, then, turning to his fellow passengers and smiling at his audience, he barked, a little too loudly, "Good Morning!"

As he sat down, hugging his black metal lunchbox to his ample stomach, his tiny bird-like eyes took in every passenger. He hoped to catch someone's eye and start a one-sided conversation. Larry was proud of his job and enjoyed telling people about it.

Nope, no one new, he thought, as everyone knowingly avoided looking at him.

His attention flitted from the people on the bus to the defaced pictures just above the windows, and finally, out the window to count the traffic lights. When the bus approached his familiar stop, Larry pulled the irritating buzzer. As he made his way to the door, the other passengers stared at him, some coldly, some smiling in amusement.

Not glancing back, swinging his lunchpail at his side, he walked straight ahead toward the employees' entrance, as he had done every weekday for the past four years. Once in the hospital, Larry went first into the laundry, then to the ground floor Men's Room to change into dull blue "scrubs" with drawstring pants. His fellow workers hated wearing them, but the uniform made Larry feel like an important part of the hospital staff. It was one of the little things that gave him a sense of belonging.

Staring out the open bathroom window at the adjacent parking lot, he watched Angie get out of her rusty old VW. She waved to him, but he just stood there, as if in a trance. Angie often wondered what he was thinking about as he stood, without moving, squinting his eyes. Humming, she came into the laundry room just as Larry returned, wearing his hospital scrubs. Larry always felt his day was going according to schedule when Angie showed up.

Good old Angie! The one person, aside from his mother and a few kids, who was kind to him. He wasn't sure why—maybe because she, too, was overweight and had pimples. Angie always took time to explain things to him, especially about the latest book she was reading. Once she even gave him a book to keep. He didn't understand why she was giving him a present, but she had patted his hand and told him he was better than the rest of the crew because he worked hard and did more thinking. He didn't understand the thinking part, but after that he worked even harder, so Angie would always be proud of him.

A few minutes later Joe and Tom walked in. As usual, they were snickering about a girl they had passed in the hallway. They were always making jokes about girls, but they never teased Angie, because she didn't go along with their crudeness. She had an unspoken dignity that somehow put her above them. Instead, they waited for Larry, who was willing to be the butt of their jokes in exchange for feeling like one of the gang.

"Hi, Larry." Angie smiled at him, ignoring the other two.

"Hi, Angie, wanna kiss?" Larry had heard Tom greet one of the delivery girls that way yesterday. He puckered up, his buck teeth protruding.

"No Larry," she replied, quickly stepping out of the huge man's way, before he had a chance to kiss her or pick her up and drop her into a laundry bin to show off for the guys.

"Who'd wanna kiss those dog lips?" Tom joked to Joe.

"Dog lips *and* dog breath," Larry retorted, as if he were part of their private joke. He cocked one bushy eyebrow and they all roared, all except Angie, who walked away.

Larry patted his shaved head and resumed his work. That would show them he was a good sport.

"What a retard," Joe giggled, nudging Tom. Just for an instant, Larry's eyes clouded over, as if he realized they were making fun of him. He took his job seriously, but to the other three it was just a summer lark. Larry wanted so badly to be like them. Angie was smart, Tom and Joe were clever and cool. Despite their teasing, they made work lively, if only for a few months.

Just then the Housekeeping Supervisor walked in, announcing, "I need some extra help today. Who's going to wash the walls?"

Tom and Joe pretended not to hear. Angie continued intently folding laundry.

"I will," Larry responded. Maybe now they'd appreciate him. He was always willing to take on more than his workload.

"Fine." As the supervisor turned to go, he called over his shoulder, "By the way, you'll have to wear a mask, gown, and gloves. It was infectious."

For an instant everyone stopped what they were doing and looked at Larry. The large towel Angie was folding slipped quietly to the floor. Tom nudged Joe, who began to smirk.

"No problem," Larry quipped, remembering a line he had frequently heard.

Larry really didn't mind washing walls. The smell of the strong cleaner was comforting to him. It was much better than the sour smell of some of the things he had to do here. It reminded him of home and his elderly mother. She was forever cleaning, cooking, and fussing over him. He was her only child.

Larry would have been content to spend his adult life at home with his mom, letting her dote on him, but his guidance counselor had said he was perfectly capable of working a simple job. In that way he could feel productive. Larry wasn't sure what productive meant. He thought it meant useful. Was he useful? He looked down at the bucket of dirty water and dipped the rag in and out, scrubbing hard.

Larry tried to help his mom around the house, even though he didn't understand how some things worked. And he enjoyed goofing around with the neighbor kids. His mom was always reminding him that he didn't know his own strength and could hurt one of them. But he knew he would never do that to any living creature. As much as he disliked spiders and bugs, he understood that they too had a right to be there without a big bully squashing them. Hurt someone? Never! Besides, he knew bad guys got punished, and he didn't want to be punished. He just wanted to be like everyone else.

The change in routine threw Larry off. By lunch-time he was crabby and he found it irritating that he had to return to the basement to pick up his lunchbox.

"Hey, Lar, we missed you," Tom called, as Larry walked into the cafeteria.

Larry puffed out his massive chest. They missed him! He sat down and opened his lunchbox, unsuspecting. He took out the big thermos of milk and the three sandwiches his mom had thoughtfully packed for her "growing boy." As he reached for the last sandwich, his hand froze in mid-air. There on the bottom of his lunchbox, right next to his homemade chocolate chip cookies, lay a small, dead baby bird.

Larry swallowed hard, fighting to keep a bitter taste from coming up in his throat. Tom and Joe exchanged a quick look.

Suddenly, Larry realized what had happened: They had done this to him. Even Angie, who had been concentrating on a book, looked up at the two boys suspiciously.

"Hey, Lar, what's for lunch?" Tom asked slyly.

Joe touched his mouth with his paper napkin. "Anything special?" he added, innocently.

Larry's nostrils began to sting, as anger crept up into his face. Why did they do things like this? He tried so hard! The other day he overheard Joe imitating him and Tom saying, "He's not smart enough to do that—he's a 'retard.'"

Should he show them that retarded people could laugh and take a joke? Maybe he wasn't as smart as college boys, but he had feelings too. They should know that.

"What's the matter, Larry?" asked Angie. She seemed concerned, almost the way a big sister would be, even though Larry was at least a foot taller than she.

Obviously, she didn't know what was in his lunchbox. Joe and Tom could hardly contain themselves; Joe was biting his lower lip; a sound gurgled in Tom's throat, as if he was choking.

Larry looked inside the box again. The bird's short gray-brown fluff seemed so soft, so vulnerable. He wanted to touch it. Its tiny claws reminded him of the parakeet he once had. Its claws had tickled when it would perch on Larry's ten-year-old finger.

One day he had felt sorry for the parakeet, living in a cage with only a sandpaper perch, a water and feed trough, and a mirror. It seemed so lonely. So he opened the cage and set it free. His mom had been furious, insisting that the bird couldn't live on its own. The outside world would be a terrifying jungle to a bird that had lived all of its life in a cage. But Larry was sure his parakeet had felt a thrill of being free, as it fluttered excitedly out the door. His mother sometimes reminded Larry of that mistake when he wanted too much independence for himself, but he never regretted what he had done.

Kind of like a kid sailing downhill on a new bike, eyes shining with new-found freedom; that feeling of being almost out of control, of his stomach still up in the air, while he was already crashing at the bottom. If he'd known the ending, would he have taken the joyride?

"So what's in there?" Joe's voice interrupted Larry's remembering.

Larry's mind could again hear Tom's mocking voice, whispering, "retard." A tic started at the corner of his mouth. He had the urge to smash Tom's nose, but he knew that would be "bad."

Instead, he looked down at the bird and gently placed his napkin over it, while he tried to think. Angie had said he was a good thinker. What would she do if this happened to her? She wouldn't get mad and lose her cool. She'd know just what to say to make life normal again. Well, he could try.

"Gee, just the good lunch my mom packed," he replied innocently, forcing himself to take a bite of his sandwich.

Tom and Joe's giggles subsided and lunch ended on a quiet note. Larry was the first to slowly push himself from the table, stand up, and leave.

"Larry," Angie called, just as he was shoving his lunchbox onto an empty shelf in the laundry room. "Larry, listen to me."

He turned toward her, his face reflecting his utter dejection.

"What did they do?" she asked, gently touching his shoulder.

"They put a dead bird in my lunchbox." His thick eyebrows bushed together in anger.

"Oh my God, that's sick." Angie closed her eyes. "Are you sure they were the ones that did it?"

As the two college boys walked in, chattering together, Larry's accusation was confirmed. They took one look at Angie and Larry and immediately stopped talking. Joe went red, and Tom looked quickly away.

Later, when Larry glanced up from the garment pressing machine, he saw Angie, her back to him, talking to Joe and Tom. Her gestures were quick, stabbing the air. He couldn't hear what she was saying but he saw the boys nod their heads, looking ashamed. He thought sadly of the soft little bird, still resting in his cold steel lunchbox.

At break time Angie came over and shared her candy bar with Larry. They sat on the wooden bench, the smell of the just-laundered clothes somehow freshening the stuffy room. Joe and Tom stood off to one side, pretending to talk, but watching them out of the corners of their eyes.

"Larry," Angie whispered, "they admitted doing it. Now I want you to do something for me. I want you to repeat the words that I tell you, and say them loud enough for Tom and Joe to hear. Do you understand?"

Larry looked confused, but his head nodded slightly, as he watched her pink lips move.

"I want you to say, 'Yes, the only way I can control my temper is with the pills my mom gives me. Otherwise I go *crazy.*'"

Larry looked puzzled as she repeated the words, quietly, slowly, her face looking stern. *Could he remember all that? And why should he say it? What did it have to do with the bird?*

"Did you have your medicine this morning, Larry?" Angie spoke loudly enough for the sulking boys to hear.

For just a moment, Larry hesitated. Then he plunged in. "Yes. The only way I can control my temper is with the pills my mom gives me." He said the words forcefully, but he forgot the rest.

Angie prompted him. "What happens if you don't take your pills, Larry?"

"I go *crazy!*" he shouted, suddenly remembering.

Tom and Joe stared at Larry, their mouths hanging open. Taking a step backward, Joe turned and went quickly back to work. Tom's face seemed to turn a shade paler, as he too suddenly got very busy.

"Good job, Lar," Angie winked at him. He saluted her, then marched back to the press.

At the end of the day, Larry checked his lunchbox before he left to go home. Just as Angie had predicted: no bird.

"I wonder where it went?" he mused. Then he smiled to himself, as he remembered his parakeet, flying out the door. He would ask his new friend tomorrow.

POOR DEVIL

A *VeriTale* by David Eli Shapiro

Dear Reader,

The story which follows is a trip inside the thinking of an old coot. He may be from the Old Country; he certainly has his own ways of thinking, even his own language. But don't despair! You can follow the action without knowing a word of Yiddish. For instance, a "minyan" is a quorum for prayer, or a congregation. But you didn't need to know that unless you're fond of bilingual puns. If you wonder why whenever the protagonist mentions or even thinks the name of a departed relative, he says, "Zekher livrokho," there's a glossary where you can find out that the Hebrew phrase means "May he be remembered for blessing." On the other hand, you may very well enjoy the story without looking up a single word. If so, mazel tov.

The tired old rabbi drooped wearily. He ran his fingers fretfully through his thinning beard. Khayim's mind was empty, his spirit curdled. Over what? Nothing—no one thing. Over life. So naturally, or un-naturally, with a thunderclap and a whiff of sulfur, a demon came seeking his soul.

Perhaps the visitation was a knee-jerk response from the minion of Hell, who had noticed a mortal abandoning hope. In any event, it followed customary protocol.

"What three wishes will you have?" thundered the towering, muscular, red-faced fiend—as though he were addressing a falling Christian.

Of course, he wasn't.

"You'll wait a minute," answered the ancient. Khayim had never liked demands, and this loud, rude *goyische kopf* made him irascible. One hand rubbing his shiny scalp under the edge of his *yalmeke*, he gestured with the other. "Happens you weren't expected. Was my head glued on solid, you think I'd be talking with the likes of you?"

The demon folded his arms and sat back, a small smile on his fearsome face. Maybe this client didn't realize what he was risking by considering an offer from below; or maybe the fool just couldn't resist a chance to dicker. No matter.

He amused himself by speculating. What was this one going to try? A mathematician in one of the colder Hells had come up with a list covering the possibilities. There were so few choices, really. There was the recursive, such as three more wishes. Or the paradox, such as travel back in time to cancel their conversation. Or the absurd, such as the power to rule *him*. Or the magnanimous gesture, coming from simpletons who presumed that kindness cancels corruption.

Most likely it would be the usual small greediness. He snickered silently. It didn't much matter how they played; his job was to harvest players.

The rabbi fiddled with his beard. This minion from Hell, this is any kind of *minyan* for me to join with? Well, to talk it don't hurt—is no kind of future, what I got ahead.

But what for to ask?

Better health, maybe? No. Save that one for the sick *nebbishes*.

Youth? Do I want to be panting after those young girls with their hair crazy colors? Nah, I'd be embarrassed.

Money for comforts? Heartburn and sunburn together on the Riviera, that means.

How about good friends again to *kibitz* with? That would be nice. Eh, but no one can replace the friends I've lost—Moyshe with the funny imitations, Hannele, the people I used to teach *Kheder* with.

Khayim sighed. What would my old *Zayde, zekher livrokho,* say to see his grandson in this pickle? Three times a day I pray to God. And what good it does me, I should end up like this? I thank God for this, thank God for that, not that I'm so happy what I got. I pray the same things every day, for what that's worth—God should grant me knowledge, understanding, wisdom. And here, I'm so *farblondjet* and *farchadat* I don't know what do I want.

He slapped his cheek, just as his *Zayde* used to when *parsking a shayle*. So simple it was. "Wisdom!" he pronounced firmly. "Wisdom, first of all."

"Wisdom!" the demon echoed. Khayim suddenly wondered if he'd made some horrible mistake. The demon stood up. Frowned. Sat down. Hunched forward. Then he scowled hideously, started to stand up again—and disappeared.

"What *meshugaas* is this?" the rabbi wondered. He waited. He pondered what he knew of Christian myth, and as he thought about it, understanding came.

What did this devil want? He wanted my soul. And for what? Look who he is. He wanted it for to torture. And how could he torture me once my body is finally wrapped in the *kittel*? By showing me all my foolishness: how I run, how I hide, how I lie to myself. He for sure didn't show up—or get lost, neither—because I'm such a saint.

Okay. Suppose the *putz* helped me find wisdom. Then I do what I can do, and accept already what I can't. No faking with myself just to save my feelings. So once I'm getting like that, what could he do me that's so terrible? For him really I didn't offer no bargain.

That's how the rabbi thought. Poor devil, he thought. For, you see, it wasn't *pilpul* logic that gave Khayim a chance to find wisdom. Knowledge and understanding are the start, but they never bear the fruit of insight without something the rabbi already had: compassion . . . and a little humor.

Feeling compassion for the unfortunate fiend made room for a little compassion toward himself—something he had mislaid.

The rabbi stroked his beard more gently than before. He hummed a little *nigun*. Life wasn't so bad, really.

GLOSSARY

Farblondjet: bewildered and off-track.

Farchadat: confused.

Goyische Kopf: Gentile head, literally. Not dunce, exactly; used more for someone who can't comprehend Jewish ways.

Khayim: man's name, accurately transliterated; usually anglicized "Chaim." The nearest English equivalent is Charles, but literal translation of the word "khayim" is "life," unlike "Charles," which means "manly."

Kheder: religious grade school.

Kibitz: engage in small talk with an element of humor or teasing.

Kittel: burial shroud (also worn during Day of Atonement prayers).

Mazel tov: Congratulations; literally, Good Luck.

Minyan: congregation; technically, quorum for prayer.

Meshugaas: craziness.

Nebbishes: pitiful persons.

Nigun: semi-devotional melody, traditionally wordless.

Parske: resolve dialectically.

Putz: Jerk.

Pilpul: dialectic.

Shayle: question.

Yalmeke: skullcap.

Zayde: grandfather.

Zekher livrokho: "of blessed memory."

REQUIEM

A Veri-tale by Sharlie West

They had been fishing all day on one of those eight-hour boats that go way out in the ocean, promising the big ones to anyone who has patience . . . and a strong stomach.

Anne Morgan spent most of the time below deck, reading magazines and wishing she had stayed in her room. She could handle the water from a distance, but not when it was directly in front of her. Her husband, Tom, sat sullenly on deck, scowling at the waves as though ordering a fish to jump on his line.

The fish, however, refused to cooperate, and teasingly jumped up out of the water just out of reach. Anne was relieved when the long afternoon ended. The moment they docked she climbed off the boat onto the pier, glad to be back on the shore. Tom walked along beside her, shaking his head. "The boat next to us had twelve strikes; I counted them. Our guy just didn't know what he was doing or where he was going. You have to follow the birds. He wasn't following the birds, he just went any way he felt like going."

"Well, maybe we can have fish for dinner," Anne replied, trying to get him out of a bad mood. "There's a restaurant on the top floor of the hotel."

"We're going over to Bill and Julie's for dinner. I ran into Bill last night in the Osbourne Building lounge. He was glad to see someone from ICA's main office, said he was going stir crazy here on the island."

Anne didn't know Julie and Bill, and she had no idea what to wear. She finally decided on a gold and white Hawaiian dress she had bought the day before, short and slit up the sides. Her long sandy blond hair was dry from the sea air, so she broke open a vial of conditioner and combed it through. She looked at her reflection in the mirror—tall, slender, long waisted and long legged, definitely not built for the island styles.

"What are they like?" she asked, as Tom was taking the tags off a blue silk shirt, hand-painted with ancient warriors. The shirt seemed to suit his dark hair and sharp blue eyes.

"Bill and Julie? I don't know. They have four kids. He's big on golf, plays every day he can."

"Does this look all right?" she asked, turning around.

Tom gave her a perfunctory glance. "You look fine. Come on, we're late."

They drove in silence to the Ilikai Hotel and took an elevator to a tenth story apartment overlooking the ocean. The door was opened by a short, thin man with a wide grin. Behind him stood a plump woman wearing no make-up, jeans, and a flowered shirt. "Good to see you both. Come on in. Anne, I don't think we've met. I'm Bill Catlin, and this is my wife, Julie."

As they entered the apartment, Anne glanced quickly around the living room. About twenty people, all dressed in shorts and jeans. Bill brought over two tall glasses, each containing a frosted pink drink with several kinds of fruit on the side. After a few minutes Tom walked away and started making his rounds, shaking hands with everyone. "Hey, Jimmy, how are you doing? Great seeing you again. Hello, Pete, you're looking good."

A tall man with a mustache and beard leaned against a wall in the corner of the living room, watching Anne as she sat down on a tan-colored couch. He was lean and muscular, dressed in a yellow shirt and khakis, with a camera slung over his shoulder. He smiled at her and walked across the room.

"John Asher," he said, sitting down next to her. "Everyone calls me Asher."

"Hello, Asher," she smiled. "I'm Anne Morgan."

"You must be Tom's wife. Let me play host for a minute while Bill's busy. Have you eaten? There's food on the table over there."

"No I haven't. I thought we were invited for dinner, so I dressed up. I really feel out of place."

"Let me get you something."

Asher walked over to a round table containing the remainders of cold cuts and rolls. He put together a good-sized sandwich and as an afterthought put a pickle on the side.

"Thanks," she said, biting into the sandwich. "We were out on a fishing boat all day and I got seasick. This is the first thing I've had to eat. So tell me about yourself. Do you work with Tom?"

"In a way. I'm a liaison between new businesses and the local establishment, which is how I met your husband. How about you?"

It was interesting how his eyes matched his hair, an amber brown with gold flecks. His mustache and beard were a deeper shade of amber, bleached in some places by the sun. Between bites she answered him.

"Not a lot to tell." She found it hard to pull away from his gaze. "I'm a free-lance writer, mostly poems and short stories, which will probably never get published. Tom thinks I'm wasting my time, that I should be in the real world more. He's right I suppose."

"Mmmm, possibly. If only to get more material."

He had moved closer to her, and sat with his body facing hers. She was very conscious of him as he was talking. *I'm the new kid on the block,* she thought, *and this is probably standard procedure.* Tom, busy talking to someone and gesturing with a cigar, half-turned his body in her direction.

"Why the camera?" she asked. "Do you need it in your work?"

"I do a lot of free-lance photography for magazines. There are some beautiful places around the islands that most tourists don't know about. Hidden waterfalls, private beaches."

She sighed, wistfully. "I wish I could see them, but this is mostly a work trip for Tom."

"I could show them to you if Tom is in meetings. Are you busy tomorrow?"

"I don't know what our plans are yet. . . ."

Asher smiled at her. "Maybe we can talk later. I hope I get to see you again before you leave. I have to go now. Fred Johnson's been trying to catch my eye. He wants to set up Friday's schedule."

He got up to leave, half-saluting her as he moved away. Anne walked over to the window and looked out at the ocean, quiet and mysterious, with the moon barely visible. *I wonder if I will see him again.*

She was startled when Tom appeared at her side. He had finished his politicking and was ready to leave.

"What were you and Asher talking about?" he asked as they left the apartment. "Did he mention ICA?"

The night air was sweet and heavy with the fragrance of flowers; she could almost taste it. *I could live here and be happy,* she thought. *It suits my soul.*

"Anne . . . did you hear me?"

"Oh . . . yes . . . Nothing, really. He was just . . ."

"Just . . . ?" he said, annoyed at what he called her "drifting sentences."

"Just putting me at my ease. I didn't know anyone there, you know. He didn't mention ICA."

"Good. You have to be careful here. By the way, I have to work tomorrow. Do you think you can amuse yourself?"

"Oh, sure. I'll walk around, do some shopping, spend your money."

"You're always able to do that," he said, sounding relieved.

Anne spent the next morning strolling through a shopping center near the Hilton. She found a small jewelry shop with handcrafted gems and bought a pink coral ring in the shape of rose petals surrounded by small pearls. Further down the center she spotted a swim apparel store with bright colored bikinis in the window. She went in and on impulse tried on a hot pink and green bikini. Squeezed into the tiny dressing room, she frowned at herself in the mirror. *My*

breasts are too small, she thought, *and I have too many stretch marks.*

She walked slowly back to the hotel room and turned on the television. Nothing on but the soaps. After a while she filled a glass with ice, vodka, and tonic and walked over to the sliding glass doors which led to a terrace. In the distance she could see the green layers of the ocean, blending from pale green to turquoise to a deep, dense green.

Only a few people were sitting on the beach. A small boy was building a sand castle, and the waves were lapping over it, covering his legs. Anne started to shiver. She pulled the drapes over the glass doors, sat down on the bed and wrapped her arms tight around her. Still, the shaking continued. She couldn't control it. Quickly, she swallowed the vodka and tonic, and after a while the trembling stopped. *Not here,* she thought, *please don't let something happen here. Not so far from home.*

"I'm still working on that document," Tom informed her, coming out of the shower the next morning. "Do you want to go over to the office with me, see where I hole up while you're lazing on the beach?"

"You know I haven't been on the beach, Tom. Why do you pretend that I have?" She knew her question would never be answered. "I could meet you at the office for lunch though."

"Good idea. We can all go. There's a Japanese restaurant a block away that Asher's been trying to drag me to."

He would be there.

Anne looked through her clothes carefully, considering first a soft pink shirt and matching pants. *Too much like cotton candy.* She finally decided on a blue-green halter dress, adding a pale green necklace and earrings.

As she walked into the concrete and glass Osbourne Building, she felt somehow self-conscious. Realizing that she was starting to tremble again, she inhaled slowly, counted to six, then let the air out. *Take it easy,* she told herself, *just take it easy.* Consciously relaxing her shoulders, she walked down the hall and found the ICA office suite where Tom was working.

"Hello Anne."

Asher sat relaxed in a black leather chair in the conference room, wearing a jade green shirt, tan slacks, and sandals. "I was wondering if we would get together again." He walked over and kissed her lightly on the cheek. "Sit down and talk to me while you're waiting."

Anne sat down in a leather chair across from him. Asher put his hand on the conference table, slowly walked his two fingers toward her, drew a question mark, and walked them back. Just then, Tom came out of a side office, walking quickly, and jingling the change in his pocket.

"Asher I'm having a problem with Takai, and we can't expand without his approval. I don't know why he's dragging his feet. We redid that proposal five times and then they demanded a new cost analysis. Same old same old."

For a moment Asher hesitated. "He needs some time to get used to the idea."

"He's had time. What's the reason for the stall?"

"Time's different here, Tom. And you play by their rules." Asher's eyes hooded over slightly. "There's still a degree of hostility toward outsiders."

"What?" Tom's voice jumped on the answer. When he spoke, his words were more a demand than a question. "Can you arrange an appointment with him for this afternoon?"

Anne saw Asher give an imperceptible shrug. "I'll go over to his office after lunch and see what I can do."

Tom's stride relaxed as they all walked into the Mashiko Restaurant. There were several staff members already there, seated around a long oval table facing a man-made waterfall. Tom walked around the table and found a seat next to a short, dark-haired man, wearing gold wire-rimmed glasses.

"Sit with me, Anne" suggested Asher. "Tom has to concentrate and score quick while the people here are receptive. Tomorrow they could turn him off."

Asher sat down at the table across from her, smiling, as though they were old friends. "By the way, you're not the only frustrated writer. A hundred years ago—well, five anyway—I wrote a novel."

"A novel? I'm impressed. I've always wanted to write a novel, but I don't think I could extend a story line for that long a period."

"Well, somehow I managed. And now the main character is sitting across the table from me."

"Who, me? Really? Well, I hope it's not a murder mystery."

"No, it's a love story, of sorts. You would have to read it to understand."

"I'd like to."

Asher thought for a minute. "I want you to. I could bring the book by the hotel in the morning. I'll try and set up an early appointment for Tom with Takai. If it goes through, I'll call you tomorrow, about ten."

Anne hesitated. "How will I say I got your book?"

"It would probably be better if you didn't. Pack it in your suitcase and read it later. I have several copies. We better order now. People are becoming aware of us, and this is a tight little island. Gossip is a way of life."

Anne listened to his staccato voice, picked up the menu and stared at it without seeing anything. After a few minutes Asher motioned to the waiter, who was waiting impatiently, and gave him an order for sashimi. "I'm going to leave now; that way no one will busy themselves with us. You'll like the sashimi here." He got up and walked around the table, taking time to shake hands with everyone, and to talk briefly to Tom. He did not look at her again.

Suppose for some reason Tom doesn't have a meeting this morning and comes back early? Anne was making a pot of coffee with the small Mister Coffee supplied by the hotel. *What do I know about his man?* Her hands shook as she raised a cup to her lips. Just then, the phone rang. She flinched.

"No need to worry," Asher's voice reassured her. "Tom's with Takai. It should take several hours; they're going to lunch afterwards."

"Where are you calling from?"

"Downstairs. Want some company?"

Yes, she thought, looking at her shaking hands, *I do need some company.* "Come on up."

Anne tossed through her clothes, pulled on a pair of jeans and a blue cotton shirt. Then she poured Smirnoff into a glass of orange juice and drank it down in three quick gulps. Responding to Asher's knock, she opened the door, feeling awkward and not knowing what to say.

"You look scared. Would you like me to leave?"

"No, come in. I'm just having some coffee."

He walked in and glanced around the suite appreciatively. "Great view. Here's a copy of my book, as promised."

"Would you like some coffee?"

"Not really." He looked at her empty glass. "I'll have some vodka and juice."

Anne went into the small kitchenette and busied herself making drinks. *Now what do I do?* she wondered.

Just then Asher stepped past the low counter and took the drinks from her hands. "Would you like to sit on the balcony?"

"Yes, I'd like to sit there." *I'd like to be able to.*

They sat on white plastic chairs, facing the ocean. As Anne looked at the waves crashing against the sand, she hugged her arms against her body. The waves seemed to be calling to her.

"What's wrong, Anne? You look pale."

Before she knew she was speaking, she replied. "Asher, I'm scared."

"Here, take my hand. I think we better go inside."

He led her into the room, and together they sat down on the soft rose quilt, covering the queen-sized bed. "Now, tell me what's troubling you."

In the distance she could hear the insistent sound of the waves and her own voice answering their call. "It's the ocean. I can't look at it. My . . . our . . . son drowned last year." As she spoke, she started to shake again. "I watched them pull him out of the water. I've been wanting to talk to someone for so long, but I haven't been able to. I didn't really want to come on this trip. It's too soon."

"God, no one should have to go through that. Do you blame yourself, Anne?"

She sighed and thought about it. "Yes. You know how mothers are. I should have been there and I wasn't."

"You couldn't be there all the time. It's not possible. And I suppose Tom lays the blame on you, too?"

"Yes. But he refuses to talk about it. We just pretend everything is the same, but it's not. It never will be again. You read about it happening to other people. But when it happens to you, it's like there's a wall between you and everyone else. You yell and yell and no one can hear you."

"Oh, Anne, you've been so alone. I wish there was some way I could help you."

"You are helping me."

Asher put his arms around her, drawing her into him with strength and tenderness, as though their souls were joining each other again after a long separation. Anne lay on the bed, cradled in Asher's arms, feeling as intimate as a bride with her new husband.

The sound of a door slamming down the hall intruded on the moment. "You really shouldn't stay any longer," she said. "We're taking too much of a chance." *And the longer you stay, the longer I will want you to stay.* She moved reluctantly out of the comfort of his arms. He got up slowly and kissed her goodbye, a long, gentle kiss.

"Write to me, Anne. Keep in touch with me. Tell me how you are doing, how you like the book."

After Asher left, Anne sat on the edge of the bed, still feeling his touch on her skin, knowing she would feel it for a long, long time. *I'll try and go for a walk on the beach,* she thought. *I have to try.*

She put on a black swim suit, threw a white sweatshirt over it, and went downstairs, through the lobby, and out the back entrance. She continued to walk until she reached the edge of the water. There she paused, took off the sweatshirt, and walked slowly in. The water was cold. She waded through it, one foot in front of another, as though pulling a heavy object. Minutes later . . . years later . . . the water was up to her chin. *Stay with me, Asher. Help me do this.* Then she dove in, letting the waves engulf her, going under, emerging, and diving in again, over and over again. Finally, she stood up and shook the salt water out of her hair and face.

It's a beginning, she thought . . . *like learning to walk all over again.*

The afternoon was hot and hazy. Anne heard the sounds of the Good Humor truck, just slightly off-key, several blocks away. She sat on a wooden rocker on the back porch with a book opened on her lap. SEA CHANGE, she read, *by John Asher.*

> Mike Lancaster stood at the airport, waiting for Carole Wells. He was camouflaged, as always, behind dark glasses, a mustache, and beard. He saw her at a distance, his photographer's eye recording her model-like appearance: long, blond hair, deep blue eyes, high cheekbones, a mouth short of perfection because of a too-full underlip, long legs, small breasts. . . .

It's me, she gasped. *I'm reading about myself. No, I'm reading about us, in a book written five years before we met.*

Throughout the afternoon she continued to read, closing the book only when the characters finally, reluctantly, had to part. Slowly, she rose from the chair, walked into the house, and put the book in a drawer under some old clothes. Then she started to cry, feeling an intense loss that she could hardly explain. *A sea change,* she thought. *A sudden transformation.*

Tom was in the back yard, putting the lawnmower away. "Anne," he shouted, "I almost ran out of gas. How many times have I told you to refill the can whenever it's empty. Don't you ever listen to anything I say?"

She walked to the back porch, where she stood looking at him, at his opaque blue eyes, which seemed always to look around her, never at her. *We haven't listened to each other for a long time,* she thought.

"Come inside Tom," she heard herself say. "I think it's time we had a talk."

ORIGINAL SIN

A Veri-tale by William Luvaas

My Aunt Louise wore three feathers in her hair that summer I went to live with her. "Red-tailed hawk," she said, though the feathers were tawny brown and glistened evilly from the black bun where she stuck them, conjuring in a boy's mind the commandment *THOU SHALT NOT COMMIT ADULTERY,* barked sternly by our old minister back home. I couldn't say why it should, any more than I understood the commandment's meaning.

Aunt Louise committed *Adulthood.* Mother had warned me of that often enough, but she was helpless before the necessity of bequeathing me to her. Mother had become paler and thinner through the spring, so listless she often refused to eat. By May, I cooked what few meals were taken in our house, hardly eating myself. Nobody mentioned the dreaded word, but somehow I picked it out of thin air: the smell of her vomit in the morning, hollows where her eyes had been, prescriptions I fetched from the pharmacy (Cocooned in the pharmacist's silence, the sly consolation of eyes.) Cancer. I knew.

My boyhood, which never had much of a flight, without a father to navigate it, crashed hard that spring and remained down. Innocence was soon to follow.

Actually, Aunt Louise fit more naturally into the realm of childhood than adulthood: hawk feathers and pink tennis shoes, her habit of taking Ralph, a raggedy-eared tabby cat, to bed with her, beginning each day in her bedroom next to mine profanely expelling him. "Ungrateful little shit," she'd scream. I rubbed the word's hard underside against my palate, learning it was possible—as Mother had taught me it was not—to curse without conjuring a vivid image of the word uttered. Likely Mother had little practice.

But I stood transfixed, ears pinned to sides of my head, the first time I heard Louise use the "F-word." It was a word I had never actually heard uttered—certainly not in my mother's house. I couldn't get enough of it. I practiced firing it at knickknacks in my room like a Remington hollow-point. I never missed. It made my ears burn to think of Mother lying in a hospital bed in Portland while I practiced the "F-word" in Seattle, but I was as helpless before it as some are before a slot machine. Any boy raised to believe humans are featureless beneath their clothing is at the mercy of every obscenity.

The obscenity facing Mother that summer was too filthy even for Aunt Louise's seasoned lips. I knew well enough that without drastic cause mothers like mine do not bequeath their adolescent sons to aunts like Louise. Surely, Mother would have kept me among her own people if there had been any. But she, too, was an only child, her parents dead. So in desperation, days before she checked in for her operation, she went to Louise, who had always had a soft spot for Mother and me.

"You are going to stay with your father's sister a time," she told me that last day, exhausted from the effort of sitting up in a chair, her hands icy wafers, sandwiching mine between. Their cold terrified me, as did the pulsing blue angle worms that had extemporized overnight in the hollow above her nose. "You may see some strange things, Tommy. Louise's hygiene isn't up to what you are accustomed to, she keeps odd hours, and she smokes too much." Mother's fingers clutched my elbow, her eyes the ethereal blue of a saint with only one foot in this world. "Remember what I've taught you. Trust in your own good judgment." She smiled at me with lips alkaline pale and chafed. It occurred to me then that she expected me to see strange things—that she counted on it, as she had once counted on my learning to swim at summer camp.

Aunt Louise lived alone in a narrow house on a back street of Seattle. The kitchen was flooded with light that poured in through huge casement windows and bathed the tile floor like clean white water. But the front of the house was dark and cluttered, shut away from prying eyes, heavy curtains always drawn. It seemed odd to me: my "liberal-minded" aunt, who voted for Kefauver and believed in premarital sex, living in a junk shop full of old-fashioned furniture which my Mother would have thrown out. Books, written in French or windy, strident English that reminded me of an equinoctial storm, lay on their bellies over rug and davenport, their spines broken. "Existentialists" she called them.

Her neighbors she dubbed "dirty-minded little conformists." "They'd burn me at the stake if it were legal." She dismissed them with a wave of her hand, fixing restless black eyes on me. "Whatever you do, Tommy, promise me you won't become a cruddy little go-along."

I shook my head vigorously, staring at the red rind about her cigarette filter, piled atop other cigarette butts spilling from the ashtray.

Mother said Louise was smart enough to teach college but lacked ambition. She worked nights as a supermarket cashier and hadn't much to say about college or anything that hadn't fallen into disrepute or disrepair or that wasn't threatened with extinction. Openhearted, she talked to anyone: the mailman, Fuller Brush salesmen, Paul Harvey on the radio (shrieking "Piss pot conservative" from the kitchen sink, refuting his every point as if he stood there in the room beside her). She talked non-stop to me: the Brooklyn Dodgers, the Three Stooges, the Korean War. The war worried me. After all, my dad had died in the last war. In just six years I would be old enough for the draft. Louise assured me that modern wars don't last that long. "This nuclear business has put an end to that. You can't change the male/female ratio if you kill as many women as men."

Somewhere along the line Aunt Louise had picked up a southern accent, along with the tight little bun, feathers, and purple sack dresses. She loved Elvis, knew his ring size and brand of deodorant, and every record in the order he'd recorded it. She monogrammed his slick-haired silhouette on pillow cases and sang "Hound Dog" in the shower, but confessed to me her suspicion he wasn't much in bed. "Vain men make lousy lovers." Winking in that broad way she had of making me feel privy to something generally unknown.

About the house she wore a sleeveless smock without any shape but what she gave it. I was just becoming aware of such things: my aunt's sharp breasts and bony hips. I would lean to the side—as if to catch sight of a bird passing outside—and steal, through an arm hole, a peek of a creamy breast. Once she caught me at it.

"Look at you! You're red as a beefsteak tomato." She laughed. "Hey, it's healthy to be curious. Look! nothing to hide." Louise gripped the hem of her smock as if to lift it.

"No, Ma'am!" I cried. "I don't . . . I mean . . ."

"I got your number. On the sly." She winked and ruffled my hair.

I pulled away, my cheeks burning chili hot, and went straight outside. Not to my friend Jeff's next door (who wasn't allowed on Louise's property because she said he possessed "a low moral temperament"), but to walk up and down hills, from the tops of which I caught flint blue glimpses of Puget Sound. Late that afternoon I returned through a cold drizzle, clothes damp, chill working into my bones, and moved stealthily through the gloomy living room, planning to go straight upstairs without speaking to Louise. It wasn't my fault she didn't wear proper underthings or that she undressed—as Jeff assured me she did—without closing her drapes. ("Come see for yourself. It's better than Playboy.") I tiptoed past bookshelves and lion-footed overstuffed chairs, certain I could make it to my room unnoticed and somehow survive the night without supper. But a voice snagged me from shadows.

"I was worried about you."

Louise was folded deep into the couch, barely visible, swaddled in the burgundy glow from drapes.

"Holy shit! You scared me."

"Better don't talk like that when you go home. I'll catch hell for teaching you profanity."

"You say it all the time."

"I'm free to say whatever I please, buster." She made a rustling sound, sitting up on the couch. "Your mama wrote."

"To me?"

"Listen, Tommy, you might have to stay a little longer."

I shrugged, pretending not to care. "She got out of the hospital last week."

"They've checked her back in. Nothing serious, honey. Routine." Her eyes slid away like they did when she discussed Elvis's religious beliefs or Kefauver's wife.

I sensed fog creeping up from the Sound along empty streets, ambushing buildings, filling nether regions of my aunt's huge house.

"You got to have faith, Tommy. You know I think churches are turkey piss, but I believe in rightness. I believe in faith."

"Will they open her up again?"

"Not very far." Her eyes flashed at me. "Just a little."

I envisioned a zipper in my mother's stomach that they could open and close at will. The idea scandalized me as nothing Louise said ever could.

We ate lavishly that night: corn waffles, rice with milk and sugar, Chet's turkey pot pies; our favorites. We felt like being kind to ourselves.

Next morning, when I shuffled from my bedroom to pee, I discovered Louise had left the bathroom door ajar. Another kindness? I stopped short, staring at my aunt afloat in a tub of lazily steaming water, lapping blue-green at the rim, her eyes gazing blankly upward, knobby hips breaking the surface, long black hair snaking down her stomach, clinging to her secret parts. For an instant I thought she was dead. Though I knew artificial respiration from Scouts, how could I possibly perform mouth to mouth on my naked aunt in the bathtub? Better to pretend I hadn't seen her. I had started to tiptoe away, mortified with guilt, when her corpse spoke behind me.

"You can use the toilet, honey. I won't peek."

Afterwards, neither of us mentioned the incident. At breakfast I kept my eyes focused on hawk feathers, leaning at acute angles from her bun, like TV antennas clinging to tenement roofs. This was another lesson of that summer: If two people ignore a thing, it's as if it never occurred. The world is not as black and white a place as I was raised to believe.

On that basis I accepted Jeff's offer to stay the night at his house. Louise thought it a splendid idea. "We could use time off from each other, don't you think?"

Later that night, when she returned from work, Louise sniffed us out as we peeked into her bedroom window from Jeff's window next door, facing hers on the second floor. Her bedroom light snapped on, adding density to the hazy emptiness between houses. Louise stood at the window, looking directly across at venetian blinds behind which we huddled. Instinctively, I ducked. "She can't see nothing," Jeff huffed. "Who cares anyway?"

My aunt toyed a moment with a blouse button, then drew the shades. I breathed relief. And disappointment.

Jeff groaned. "You never told me she had a guy over there. She only closes up when she's doing it."

His imputation made me mad. "My Aunt Louise lives alone, jerk."

He looked me over with a sly tilt of the head. "I guess you don't know much down in Oregon."

I punched his shoulder, bereft of the good judgment my mother had assured me would guide a son through such predicaments. Jeff was all over me, pummeling viciously at my head, chest, groin. I swooned beneath green currents, nausea clinging like seaweed to my stomach. Jeff pinned me down with his knees and breathed sourly in my face, teeth rooted in collars of yellow tartar, then cursed and rolled away in disgust. And I rolled up in my sleeping bag on the floor, tight as a mummy, in a faint aura of dirty socks. Next morning the events of the previous night went unmentioned. Forgotten, as if they had never happened at all.

Later at Louise's I met Uncle Sam. Anyhow, he told me to call him "uncle," in a tone that brooked no disagreement. Biceps sagged down his arms like contented bellies of Dylan Thomas's uncles after a Christmas feed. A trellis of roses twined up the left forearm, enclosing in its lattice: ***Don't Tread On Me!*** Then I realized the rose vines were really snakes. Grinning a gold tooth, Sammy demonstrated how, in the crook of his right elbow, a hula-skirted girl wiggled her belly when he pumped his arm.

"He's a big ol' ship-wrecked dummy," Louise said, flopping arms over his shoulders and resting her chin on the bald center strip of his head. "His ship is in port for the week. We hoped you wouldn't mind if he came on board as our guest."

They watched, awaiting my decision. I wasn't stupid. I knew that, shipwrecked or not, men weren't supposed to cohabit with women who weren't their wives. Besides, tattooed sailors did not shack up with eggheads like Aunt Louise. I longed to return home, where women closed bathroom doors and uncles were truly uncles. It was all happening too fast: curse words, nudity, adults seeking my permission to sleep together in the house where I was summer guest.

I nodded okay. Then Uncle Sam demonstrated the manly art of arm wrestling while Louise made ham and eggs. Years later I would empathize with Sam's shipwrecked nature and wonder whether every port of call in his sailor's life offered some challenge akin to the nephew who lived with his aunt while his mother lay dying in a Portland hospital. A faltering, white-skinned, long-eyed, hay feverish boy, who, raised on simple virtues, took every word you said quite literally. Possibly in another port—Lake Charles, Louisiana or Houston, Texas—a wife hounded him to settle down and his own son grew sullen, as mistrustful of Sam, his itinerant father, as I was.

Sam tried to instill in me his enthusiasm for tattoos and fighter planes, and pointed out the naked woman on a Camel pack. (I couldn't find her, looking as I was for Louise afloat in the tub.) His sluggish blue eyes had a red crease through the retinas. Blood blisters, he explained, from some bar room brawl. He was proud of those wounds as he wasn't of his war record. That troubled me.

Sam took me fishing on the pier: a highway of wooden planks on pilings against which the black sea frothed and snarled. I loved to watch it seethe white over layered barnacles and mussels on the timbers, spill slimy green off seaweed. One day, standing beside Sam on the pier, I told how my father had died on a troop transport, torpedoed off the Philippines before he reached the fighting. Sam stood indifferently watching the gulls, his bamboo pole drooping, line bellying close to the water. He seemed unaware of it, other than to check occasionally to see if he had lost his bait. I knew he had been a bombardier, flying missions over Pacific atolls. (He rattled off odd, tongue-tickling names: Saipan, Morotai, Pelelieu.) I envisioned him squatting in the bomb bay of a B-52, knees to chest, cradling each bomb lovingly in his hands before letting it drop into jungles below, squinting aim through the red crosshairs on his eyeballs. Avenging my father. It was the thing I found to like in him.

"I saw the whole shootin' match, right on into Okinawa," he said at last. "Personally, I liquidated sixty thousand nips. You know what that does to a man? You know what he dreams about at night?"

"The Japs killed lots of people. They killed my dad."

"Yeah, sure. Sure they did." He patted a shirt pocket for the Alka-seltzer he took for his ulcer; screwing eyes tight as if swallowing molten lead.

"Don't you use any water?" I asked him.

"Tommy, I'm real sorry about your dad. Still it don't matter who they are. Nips, Russians . . . don't matter." The line click-clicking as he reeled in. "It's all human beings the same."

"The Japs killed my dad."

He looked at me, eyes gone vague and polished. Moisture burst from his lips. "What do you know about my dreams?" Wheeling on a duo of old timers strolling the pier. "Watta you know? Legionnaire bastards!" Sea gulls squealed away from his shout.

The men stood gawking at him. One led the other away by an elbow, throwing back nervous glances. Sam feinted towards them and they leapt forward in a bow-legged, geriatric sprint.

"What do any of them know about my dreams?"

A black man, fishing over the rail nearby, shook his head at me as if I were at fault somehow. When I wanted only escape. Not understanding why Louise sent me off to carry Sam's bait bucket. Disgusted to think of him sharing my aunt's bed. They tried to fool me by turning up the radio, but behind liquid rhythms of jazz I knew secret rhythms were at work. Every now and again a cry broke through—a wail, half-heard on the verge of sleep, so I couldn't be sure it didn't originate in my own unconscious.

Louise took me aside one day, eyes darting about the precincts of my room, smiling at a drawing I had done of a *Tyrannosaurus Rex*. She put an arm around my shoulders and nuzzled my head, an affection I had learned to tolerate.

"Goodness sake, you're nearly tall as me."

I knew she hadn't come to discuss my height.

"Listen, honeybunch. If this was an ideal world, wouldn't be a thing you couldn't tell your mother. But it isn't. There's things she doesn't need to know about. Things a woman of her high character wouldn't appreciate. You understand?"

"I know you have sex with Sammy," I said.

Her head shook confusion. I wondered why she could not smile without lipstick leaking onto her teeth.

"We don't all share the same convictions. Some of us need some comforting. You might learn that yourself one day. Mama doesn't need to know about Uncle Sam." Her voice gone cold and mercantile. "Maybe she doesn't get so lonely." She gripped my head in the crook of her arm and nuzzled down, grinding her chin into my scalp. I struggled free from her smell of stale deodorant and perspiration.

"Is Mother dying?" I asked.

Louise flinched. "What makes you ask such a thing?"

"You won't let me read her letter."

"It wasn't hers, honey. It was the doctor's."

"She's dying, isn't she."

"I don't believe it a minute. You'll be going home soon. You'll remember the good times we had and how you went fishing with Sammy. How about later we go to Discovery Park and ride the roller coaster and maybe you can win a blue bear at the dime toss to send home to her. Think she'd like a blue bear?"

"I'm almost grown up," I snapped, "I seen you naked in the bath tub. I've done things you wouldn't even guess."

She stared. "Well I . . ."

"You don't honor that at all."

"I was thinking about your mother. And you, Tom."

"I believe she wants it to go back like it used to be before they opened her up, when I lived at home and came to visit you for a week in the summer. And me, that's all I want."

"Me too. I'd like that." She hugged me again, the sharp point of a breast inflaming me with mixed emotions. I wanted to tell her how I'd defended her that night at Jeff's. There was too much world to hold up at once. I did not yet know the cleansing power of tears. I felt them dammed, cloistered inside of me, felt their pressure at my temples and at the back of my throat, felt them leak cautiously into my eyes and survey the landscape. But didn't let them come. Tears are final. No one needed to teach me that. They come when we have surrendered to grief and there is no turning back. I was not willing to surrender Mother, or Aunt Louise. I wanted them both.

The argument started before supper. Uncle Sam boisterous all afternoon, drinking hard from a bottle in a brown paper bag, winking at me when I looked up from baseball cards spread across the dining room rug. (I had two Hank Aarons but needed a Peewee Reese.) Drinking buddy, claimant to his lewd jokes. I wished he would go down to Silky's on the corner. Instead, he sprawled in blue jeans and buttonless work shirt on a kitchen chair, speaking to no one in particular about a scar across his belly.

"Friggin' American Legion think war's a dance around a cat house. See that!" Opening his shirt to display a glazed pink weal slashing left to right (opposite what I imagined Mother's to be).

"We've heard the story, Sammy. You're talking to yourself," Louise said.

"Legionnaire done that. I carried my guts half a block before they got me down."

"It isn't the right time and place, Sammy."

"You know what it feels like?" he asked me. "Slimy and soft like wet silk. Heavy. You wouldn't believe."

I leapt up from my cards and charged upstairs to the bathroom with a hand over my mouth, afraid I was going to be sick.

"Shuddup!" Louise shouted. "Just shuddup your idiot mouth. His mother is dying . . ." Her words trailing off.

Sammy came blubbering behind me. "Sorry, kid. Didn't mean no harm." I hid behind the bathroom door. He stumbled. Seeing my chance, I leapt past him like a cat and was gone down the stairs and out of the house.

Thinking I might hitchhike to the hospital—home, I wandered the streets, until fog moved up hills along the wide avenues from the sound and scrubbed facades of shingled houses. Cold in my sweatshirt, I started back to Louise's.

The house was quiet, as it had been that earlier time. Yet there was breathing, as though the walls themselves were alive. The chill followed in behind me. Front room clutter had spread into the kitchen—but violently. An overturned chair, Louise's blouse with two buttons missing. Silence was shattered by a single cry. Upstairs. A wavering ululant groan, going on and on, with whimpering spasms between: the sound a woman might make with her throat locked in the hands of a beefy man.

I moved fast. Grabbed the largest butcher knife from the kitchen drawer, rivets of the wooden handle pressed cold against my palm, thick blade flat against my thigh, as I took the stairs two at a time.

Louise was smart enough to leave the bedroom door ajar, so I understood that first time—the bathroom—had been practice for what she had sensed coming. A woman's intuition, Mother called it. I knelt behind the door, eyes adjusting to the differential in light, greater darkness within. Sammy straddled her, as I expected he would. Bed covers torn aside in brutal, heedless assault. His bare back faced me, quilted with hair.

He made a sound low in his throat and cast his eyes towards the ceiling. His hands slipped from her neck and gripped her shoulders, shaking. Regretting, perhaps, what he had done. I remembered reading in a Dick Tracy comic how a knife thrust six inches beneath the shoulder blade just to the side of the spinal column would plunge straight into the heart. The question was whether to go stealthily or to rush forward all at once like a football back and plunge the knife into him. I decided on the second.

He was talking again—that sotted, rambling patter of obscenity and regret. I plunged forward, knife raised over my head in both hands, screaming like an Apache Indian.

Perhaps it was Louise's eyes that made me hesitate. Not dead but alive, and gleaming as I had never seen them. Giving Uncle Sam time to pivot and catch the knife blade in his bare fist. Louise curled against the headboard, knees coiled to chest in instinctual contraction. Her eyes blinked in a feverish attempt to recall my familiarity. "No," she moaned. "Oh, no."

Sammy slid the knife from his buckled, bleeding fingers. "Your daddy must've been a Legionnaire," he said.

"I thought you choked her," I stammered.

Blood dripped from his clenched fist onto the sheet. *Sure to stain* was all I could think. Perhaps Louise thought the same. She stared dumbly. Then leapt up. Firming a hand in the matted dent of Sammy's back, she guided him downstairs to the kitchen.

I followed, gaping at those two naked adults. The wiry yet bearish man, clutching one fragile hand in the other, relinquishing it to her—dripping red over the sink—his mouth opening in a mute cry. I couldn't comprehend what had happened or how I could have done such a thing. Couldn't understand it at all. Louise wrapped a flowered towel about his palm, ripped down the middle, split ends tied in a knot over the wound: what I recognized, from Scouts, as a tourniquet.

"It's deep, Sammy," she said. "We better call a doctor."

He sucked air out of his cheeks and ran the good hand back over his scalp. His eyes rolled at me, each pupil creased, a tiny fold of red. My mouth worked to tell him I was sorry.

"Does it hurt?" I managed.

"Only when I think about it." He winked.

"We need a doctor," Louise insisted.

At that instant the phone rang. Louise seized it.

"Dr. Bailey!" She laughed surprise. "Yes, yes, he's right here with me."

She discovered me then—her free hand pestering the air with gestures of concealment—a lip corner spasming reflexive smiles, as when she imitated Elvis's "Hound Dog."

"Yes, I understand." Her eyes closed, the heavy lids. "Ohhhh," she groaned. "Oh, damn it all to holy hell."

I watched, trying to concentrate, to focus interest: deflated nipples dark as coffee, puffy body sagging towards middle-age. Not shocking or dirty in the way Jeff next door had it. Merely unexpected. Even Mother, I thought, if one saw her like the day she was born. . . . Then, before tears gripped me, it occurred that I could flee. Before it was too late. Before Aunt Louise sent the house of cards tumbling with a whack of the hand. But she had already let the phone slide into its berth, snatched up her torn blouse from the floor and slipped it over her shoulders, as if considering her informality inappropriate to the task at hand.

Sammy had vanished. That blouse with its missing buttons the only evidence he had been there at all.

119

"He'll be back," she said huskily, slipping an arm around me. "Like reincarnation. Do you know about reincarnation? Our ship departs, but it returns. I want you to believe that, Tommy. No one ever leaves for good and final."

That night she took me into her bed and held me close, explained that some lessons come when one is too young to receive them. Death always arrives too young. Nestled against the loaf of her belly, I understood my Aunt Louise was a living metaphor. In her person she had condensed life and offered it to me as a gift. Perhaps that is why mother had sent me to her, knowing her chances. Strong diseases require strong remedies. All night I lay awake, while her chest rose and fell. I wondered what I had done that God should punish me so severely: that I should thieve life from the one who had given it to me.

"Mama's dead," I said when Louise woke beside me next morning.

Ill-humored to find me in her bed, eyes gritty with sleep, she shooed me out as she did Ralph, but gently.

"How would you like to live with me?" she asked later. "Maybe we could adopt each other."

She promised—as soon as she could do so without breaking down—to tell me how Mama passed away.

"There will have to be rules," she told me, after grief had come like a prodigal father returned from a long absence. Taunted and reduced me to bone in clean, pure sunshine. And when it left, I was weak and new-footed, making my way through a bleak but acceptable terrain.

"No more sleeping in my bed; you're too old for that. You make breakfast, I'll make dinner. You can do housework when you can't stand the mess any longer. Do your homework every night. And in cases where her judgment and mine conflict, you will honor your mother. First and foremost, you will always be her son."

A Secret Place

A Veri-tale by Beverly Sheresh

*Ellen awoke early that morning, certain that she had
heard someone playing the piano downstairs,* distinct
notes, rising, falling, converging . . . one of Bach's
fugues. But the house was quiet. The only sound the
call of a scrub jay out back and the distant hum of
traffic on the freeway. Later, as she sipped her coffee,
she noticed how the sun brightened the three pink
carnations she had plunked in a tumbler of water
yesterday. Somehow, her weed-ridden garden had
weathered her neglect, and she had plucked them
from a certain doom while the dew still clung to their
petals.

She wondered how long it had been since she
had really looked at anything with her artist's eye.
Exhilaration filled her, with the clarity and wonder she
had once known. Ellen wasn't sure why this was

happening to her now, this feeling, after almost a year. Like a dormant seed, it had sprouted within her, pushing its way to the light. To be outside, among flowers and trees . . . to be close to the water, where she could smell the sea . . . and to be painting again! That was what she wanted.

In the spare room at the back of the house she pushed aside old boxes of National Geographics and jig saw puzzles and bumped against discarded chairs, *sans* seats, until she found her easel. Covered with dust and cobwebs, it was behind their old piano. Ellen and her mother had never been able to part with the aging upright, even though its felt hammers were moth-eaten and most of the ivory covers for the keys were missing. "The secret place" she and her mother had called this room. When the time would come to replace the irreplaceable, her mother would whisper, "Let's hide it in the secret place," and little by little, they had put bits and pieces of their lives out to pasture.

In a box near the easel she found her art supplies, the Milton Bradley watercolors, her brushes and art paper. After gathering them up, she filled an old mayonnaise jar with water, then lugged everything outside and piled it in the back seat of her VW.

Up to now she hadn't thought of Luke. In a couple of hours, the 49er's game . . . for him, a big thing. Popcorn already popped, coke in the fridge . . . everything ready. She just couldn't wait . . . he would understand. She decided not to call him . . . he might talk her out of this. Brushing aside a touch of guilt, she wrote a note on the back of a Sears sales slip and fastened it to the door with scotch tape.

"Luke, I'll be down at the park . . . by the fig tree. Ellen."

As the car rattled down the street toward the park, she tried to think only of what she wanted to do, of what had lain hidden within her too long. But Luke was in her thoughts.

They had met about a year ago, both working as accountants for Santa Barbara County. Ellen found the work stifling, precise, not her kind of work at all, but she had grasped it willingly. It provided a refuge from thinking about the loss of her mother; from painful memories, like the arthritis that had crept into her mother's fingers until she could play the piano no more. After that, the older woman spent much of her days sitting at the window, her hands quiet in her lap. And so, for Ellen, the ledgers and trial balances, the debits and credits, filled her mind, providing a kind of surcease.

Then one day she and Luke started talking in the hall at lunch time. She was surprised that they had hit it off so well. She had always been withdrawn, living in her soft world, where there was no place for harsh realities. But Luke drew her out, making her laugh when she needed to laugh. She discovered that his was a world of "third down and two to go," "double plays" and "slam dunks." He loved most sports, but football was his favorite; and he had been so patient with her, explaining football terms and plays. But when she would comment on the games, she always seemed to say the wrong thing, stupid things.

Their relationship had been strained more than once because they were so different. It didn't seem important at first, though they were from two separate worlds. Ellen was raised in a house that vibrated with classical music, and covering the walls were paintings by Cezanne, Van Gogh, Manet, Degas . . . all impressionists . . . the kind of art she loved. Luke had never mentioned the paintings. He was from a small town in Nebraska, a farm boy transplanted into California soil, with limited interests, or so it seemed.

Still, she sensed something intangible about Luke that drew her to him.

Ellen parked the VW on a back street near the park where, in the distance, she could clearly hear the ocean surf. Just across the road stood the fig tree, the one she drove by every day on her way to work, the place where she and Luke often sat at lunchtime, munching their tuna sandwiches.

Gathering her supplies from the back seat, she crossed the street and set up her easel under the tree. Such a magnificent tree. Now, joyfully, with her child's eyes she looked at it anew—at its massive limbs, reaching out and up, and its grey trunk, scored and scarred like the hide of an ancient elephant. Ellen took a deep breath, realizing that she was happier than she had been for a long time.

A spread of bright lavender ice plant, dazzling in the sunlight, grew nearby. Just beyond stood an old wooden bench. They would make excellent subjects, she decided. After making a brief sketch, she mixed a light blue wash for the background. As she worked, the brush felt good in her hand.

While she waited for the wash to dry, Ellen pulled off her glasses, rubbing the sides of her nose. To her myopic vision the ice plant was a blur of color, like much of Monet's work . . . and she liked the effect. She decided she would paint it just that way.

Feverishly, she mixed and remixed colors, trying to capture the lavender tones. Totally lost in her work, she was startled when someone gripped her shoulders and kissed her on the back of the neck.

"Luke! You scared me!"

"Blindsided you," he said, grinning, "Lucky you didn't get sacked!"

My football hero, she thought. She couldn't help smiling as she pushed him away, but his being there made her feel uneasy.

He was much taller then she, with a thin hard body and wheat-colored hair that was already thinning on top, even though he was only thirty-four. He wore horn-rimmed glasses that Ellen had always liked. They made him look studious, and the effect pleased her.

"Brought some cinnamon rolls from Frimples," he said, waving a paper sack.

She wasn't hungry.

Choosing her words carefully, she asked, "Luke, would it be okay if we warmed them up a little later . . . in the micro?"

He hesitated for a moment then nodded. "Sure. Why not?" he said, as she turned back to her work.

She began painting the ice plant portion of the drawing. Luke stood behind her, quietly watching.

"You never told me you liked to paint."

"I thought I had. It's been a while, since I've done anything."

The leaves of the fig tree shuddered in a breeze that moved over the ice plant, making waves in a lavender sea. To Ellen the quiet was so intense that she could plainly hear the sound of her brush on the paper.

"Have you ever tried oils?" he asked.

She felt a prick of anger, certain that he was unimpressed with what he saw. Typical.

"I prefer watercolors." Then, sensing her own harshness, she added, quickly, "It's what I like . . . what I know."

Ellen remembered when as a child she had first painted with watercolors. Sitting at the kitchen table, with a big jar of cloudy water filled with brushes between them, she and her girlfriend, Marie, would copy pictures from calendars or winter scenes from

Christmas cards. Later, outside, along the coast, buffeted by the salty ocean air, that straightened their hair and stung their cheeks, they painted seascapes. When she brought her work home, her mother would clasp her hands and say, "Oh, Ellen, it's beautiful."

It had been a day just as this, in November, with the air breathing a subtle coolness, when her mother had died, slipping away with a sigh as Ellen clutched her hand. A vivid, painful memory that would not fade.

Standing behind her with his hands on his hips, Luke didn't speak for a long time. He was making her nervous. When she sighed heavily, he backed off.

He leaned against the fig tree, touching its trunk and looking up through its branches. For some time he was unusually quiet. Then he said, "Look, why don't I go back to your place . . . I'll watch the game . . . get out of your hair." He plucked a leaf, examining it, running his fingers over its surface. He didn't look at her.

She felt relieved. "Okay . . . yes." She dug her housekey from her purse.

"I'll be back a little later."

He took the key from her, squeezing her hand first. She smiled up at him. "I shouldn't be long," she said.

After watching him amble to his car, waving once from a distance, Ellen went back to work. From time to time people stopped to watch, peering over her shoulder. No comments. Maybe they were being polite. One old man in baggy pants and a flannel shirt, buttoned to the chin, watched her for a long time. He smelled of pipe tobacco and tomato soup. Pulling a toothpick from his shirt pocket, he popped it into his mouth, shifting it with his tongue from one corner to the other. She couldn't help but glance at him now and then. His not saying anything worried her, and doubt, cold and sobering, crept into her mind. She was glad when he finally left.

Ellen wanted to believe that it didn't matter, that now, she painted only for herself. Yet she knew things would never be as they were before, before her mother died. Now she needed others to see, and she hoped they would like what they saw.

When she finished, when she stepped back to look at her work, it was all that she had wanted . . . the color and light, the illusion of forms. *Oh, Mom,* she thought, *I wish you could see this.*

It was only then that Ellen noticed how late it was. Subtle color changes in her subjects. She should have realized. Hurriedly, she gathered up her supplies.

She urged the VW up Milpas Street, where eucalyptus shadows stretched across her path and the bright reds of the bougainvillea along the way had deepened to a dark crimson. She dared not look at her watch. Her stomach tightened as she thought of Luke, suddenly realizing how important he was to her.

When she finally pulled into the driveway, she found Luke sitting on the front steps, surrounded by a group of bouncing sparrows so numerous that the ground at his feet seemed to be moving.

What a relief, to see him there. He hadn't left! When she stepped from the car, the sparrows rose like a cloud, settling in a eugenia hedge near the house.

"They love cinnamon rolls," he said. But he didn't smile.

She started to apologize for her lateness, but something about the way he looked stopped her. He was making her feel guilty for something she hadn't intended, and she found that hard to forgive. Gripping her easel under her arm, she maneuvered the rest of the painting supplies with some difficulty.

Would you get the door, please?" she asked with a cool politeness.

He didn't offer to help, but he got up slowly, holding the door open for her.

"Where's your painting?" he asked.

She dropped her supplies on the kitchen table, turning to look at him, surprised that he had asked about it.

"It's on the front seat of the car. I didn't want to crush it. I'll get it," she said, sweeping past him. She felt strangely nervous about his seeing it.

When she came back, she was out of breath, and her hands were sweating as she propped the picture against the sugar bowl and the napkin holder.

He looked at it for a long time before saying anything, squinting, standing back, leaning close. Her heart thumped and her mouth felt dry. She could hear her mother's soft voice saying, "Oh, it's beautiful, Ellen." She had always been able to depend on those words from her mother. Now she realized that she wasn't really sure if her work was good. This was Luke, who would say exactly what he felt, regardless of the consequences. That was his way.

"It's sorta like the way flowers look to me when I'm not wearing my glasses." He glanced at her quickly, then looked back at the painting. "But . . . I like it . . . I like the colors . . . it looks like the flowers are moving."

Ellen grabbed his arm. "Oh Luke! That's what you're supposed to see—the movement." She could hear her voice shaking. "I wanted you to like it, I wanted that so much!"

He stared at her, obviously surprised at her outburst. As was she. It was so unlike her, to say exactly what she was feeling, holding nothing back. It felt like a window thrown open in a room closed too long, freshening the air. The feeling frightened her, but she resisted the urge to close it once more.

She slumped into a kitchen chair, feeling her throat tighten, realizing she had never really given Luke a chance. He sat down across from her, studying her.

"You know," he said, "I really wanted to stay and watch you. But, I didn't think you wanted me there."

He was right, of course.

She didn't know what to say as he sat studying her. The buzz of the electric clock and the hum of the refrigerator seemed uncommonly loud.

Luke left early that night. She didn't try to stop him. She let him go, sensing that she had hurt him, that he needed some time to himself. They hadn't quarreled. Maybe if they had, it would have cleared the air. She only knew, at this moment, with absolute clarity, how much she needed him.

For a long time after he left she sat in the kitchen, facing the painting that still sat propped on the table. She hoped it was good. But, somehow, it didn't seem that important any more. Finally, she turned off the light to sit in the dark . . . to think without distractions.

Later, before she went to bed, she opened the door to the spare room and snapped on the light. A yellow glow illuminated the old piano, the discarded furniture, the boxes, dusty and misshapen, filled with shadows of the past. She didn't need it anymore—this *secret place*—not to remember the good things. The room would be cleared . . . for a place to paint, perhaps . . . or for a place to watch football games on a Sunday afternoon.

RETURN TO SENDER

A Veri-tale by Terry Wolverton

The package arrived in one of those jiffy envelopes, slightly padded and stapled at one end. Her neighbor had signed for it. It was sticking out of her mailbox, forcing the lid open and allowing rain to soak through the entire stack of bills, catalogues, and charity requests.

This alone was enough to make her grumpy, but Ericka was truly annoyed when she glanced at the return address. "Spivack, 44 W. 12th Street, New York, NY." Dexter Spivack, she thought bitterly. What the hell could he want with her?

Once she had turned the key in the door and entered the overheated environment of her tiny guesthouse, she dumped the package with all the rest of the soggy post in a heap on her bed. She hung up her coat, scooped some cat crunchies into Blaze's yellow dish, turned on a lamp, went to the toilet, and listened to her phone messages before allowing herself to think about the package.

Even then, when she turned to the mound of mail and noticed that a sodden advertising circular was bleeding black newsprint onto her satin comforter, she still ignored the package. She sorted the whole stack into: "Personal/Must Read," "Bills/Open Later," "Junk Mail/But Looks Interesting," and "Straight to the Trash." This last pile she gathered up and without another thought dumped into the overflowing garbage pail in her kitchen.

Then Ericka returned to her bed and opened a letter from her friend Eileen, who was traveling around in South America. The rain could have turned this into a disaster, but fortunately, Eileen had written in pencil. Although thoroughly soaked, the letter was still readable. Ericka scanned the tiny, neat lines, but her concentration was spotty. It appeared her friend was having some kind of romance with a Brazilian athlete, but Ericka couldn't seem to follow the thread of it. She'd have to go back to it later.

The next envelope contained a rejection of three poems she had sent to a literary magazine seven months earlier. She quickly set the Xeroxed letter aside.

That was it for personal mail. She scrupulously avoided the jiffy bag. Instead, Ericka opened her bills, glancing at the totals and in rare cases the details, even taking time to write their due dates on the outside of the envelopes before scooping them up and stuffing them into a bulging file folder marked "Bills to Pay."

That left the catalogues. Ericka decided she was hungry, so she relocated to the kitchen, where she heated a can of soup and made toast, which she slathered with butter. This meal she ate standing against the kitchen counter, while she thumbed through four-color catalogues of housewares, garden supplies, and lingerie. After examining her bills, Ericka had decided not to buy anything more for a long time, but a set of jet black dishware caught her fancy and she decided to save the catalogue in case her resistance lowered at some future date.

It was only after polishing off the soup and toast, washing and drying the dishes, and making herself a cup of raspberry tea that Ericka finally returned to the bedroom and the package from Dexter Spivack. She considered returning her phone messages first, but finally, curiosity won out over distaste.

She grabbed the package and began trying to rip the staples out with her fingernails, completely ignoring the red tab that instructed, "Pull Here to Open." She was gleeful in her outrage when she broke one of her nails in the process. That Dexter never had been anything but trouble.

Ericka met Dexter Spivack on a tour through the Grand Canyon. Ericka was not the sort of person to seek out guided tours; in fact, it was the first and last one she had ever been on and she had been with her mother. Ericka had just graduated from college and was about to move from San Francisco, where she had grown up, to Los Angeles to try to get a job in the film industry. Her mother felt bad about Ericka's leaving home for good, as well as about her moving to Los Angeles—where the Manson clan had murdered all those people and the air was so unhealthful—and had insisted that they take this trip together.

The tour involved overnight camping, a lot of hiking, and rafting down the Colorado River. It was not the sort of trip that either Ericka or her mother was inclined toward. Ericka figured the empty nest syndrome had driven her mother to temporary insanity, but what was *her* excuse?

Anyway, Dexter had been part of the same tour group. What he was doing there was anyone's guess. In the years she had known him Ericka had asked him many times, and he invariably, infuriatingly responded, "I was there to meet you."

Her mother loved him, partly because he was so polite, and partly because she knew, with that unerring sense only mothers have, that Ericka would never be interested in him. Ericka was not. Even on first meeting she thought he was a creep. She had known him for over a year before she learned that he wore glasses not because he needed them, but because he felt they made him look more intelligent. But by that time Ericka didn't have the heart to tell Dexter that those tortoise shell frames against his pale freckled skin made him look like a geek.

Part of the problem was that Dexter wasn't very intelligent, though he desperately wanted to be. He read everything, from news magazines to gossip columns to science texts, and then elaborately flaunted misinformation in front of people who knew better.

The other problem was that he had an indefatigable ego that allowed him to relentlessly pursue women who had absolutely no interest in him.

Ericka had been just such a woman. Although she had disliked him on the tour and had conspicuously avoided his attentions, although she had given him no personal information about herself beyond her name, as soon as she moved into her new apartment in Studio City she'd gotten a call from him. As her rotten luck would have it, Dexter Spivack lived in Los Angeles, and her mother had been only too grateful to have someone she trusted look in on Ericka, all alone in that horrid city.

Dexter was the kind of man who had been turned down so often by women that "No" was meaningless to him. He simply had nothing to lose.

After his fifth phone call, Ericka had reluctantly agreed to go out with him. She was surprised by his car —a Jaguar, British Racing Green—and astonished to learn that he held a high-level position in his father's investment firm. Dexter was ready and able to wine and dine Ericka in high style. That didn't make him more attractive to her. Ericka cared about aesthetics, not money. His pretenses at sophistication were laughable to her, and his persistence was downright annoying.

After his seventeenth phone call Ericka went out with him a second time. In between he had sent her flowers, a singing telegram, and a bunch of balloons. She was working as a secretary for a small producer of B-movies—hardly the break into film she had imagined for herself. She found Los Angeles a hurried, disconnected city without neighborhoods or communities. People socialized either around work or around self-improvement, be it compulsive exercise or gurus. Dexter was the only person in L.A. who was calling Ericka.

Even today she couldn't quite figure out how he had become her boyfriend. Sometimes to a girlfriend she'd joke, "Well, he had a good job and a Jag!" To her mother she'd fume, "It's all your fault!" Or once to her therapist she confessed, "I guess he was a reflection of my self-esteem at that time in my life."

Her feelings for Dexter never changed. She wasn't attracted to him, she didn't respect him. He could afford to take her anywhere she wanted to go, but she was embarrassed to be seen with him. Did she only imagine that his friends regarded her with a mixture of curiosity and pity? Was she conscious of the fact that she avoided making friends so she wouldn't have to introduce them to Dexter? Still, in the first years that Ericka lived in Los Angeles, Dexter Spivack was the only man she dated.

She kept insisting that she wasn't in love with him, but Dexter always cheerfully reassured her that in time she would learn to. Meanwhile, he took her out to expensive dinners, to the theater or the symphony or the opera, three times a week (her limit—he would have taken her out every night). He took her on wonderful trips, week-end getaways to Palm Springs or Tahoe, vacations in the Caribbean. He was never less than utterly adoring of Ericka. And he made surprisingly tender love to her whenever she would allow it.

It was the perfect relationship with the wrong person. She couldn't stand him and it made her furious with herself that she put up with him. The night in Laguna when he presented her with the most gorgeous diamond ring Ericka had ever seen and asked her to marry him, she knew the time had come to make a stand.

She refused the ring, politely but firmly. Then she refused to see him again. For three weeks he called her every hour, around the clock, at home and at work. At night she heard his froggy pleas, emanating through the speaker of her answering machine. She took none of the calls. He called her mother, who attempted to intervene on his behalf until Ericka threatened to stop taking her mother's calls as well. She moved to a new apartment and got an unlisted telephone number. She changed jobs. She enrolled in the EST training and joined a gym. She lost herself in a city where it was easy to get lost.

She heard no more from Dexter Spivack after that. She knew he had called her mother for years, but Ericka had given her mother the most unambiguous instructions about never telling Dexter how to find her. One day, maybe six years ago, she had run into someone who knew him, who told her Dexter had moved to New York.

Obviously, he was still there. Ericka once again studied the return address. Although it had been almost ten years since she'd seen him, she could still recognize that crazed, loopy handwriting of his.

How the hell had he found her? In the intervening years she'd given up her dreams of a film career. She'd given up her search for the perfect relationship or the right person. She'd given up exercise and EST. She'd moved to this little guesthouse in Silverlake and become an occasionally published poet and a temp office worker.

Just get it over with, she told herself, sticking her hand cautiously into the envelope, as though something inside would bite her. She pulled out a rectangular box, taped shut, about the size of a six-hundred-page novel, but much lighter. Ericka held it up to her ear and shook it hard; the contents rattled slightly.

She used one of her remaining fingernails to slice through the tape on each side of the box, and lifted the lid. Inside were crumpled sheets of the *New York Review of Books*. Ericka shook her head. Same old Dexter, trying to impress her with packing material. Underneath the newsprint was a small black box.

As she picked it up, she began to tremble. She had seen this box before. Ericka flipped open the hinged lid. There in a pool of black velvet sat the diamond engagement ring that Dexter had once presented to her in the restaurant of the Ritz-Carlton Hotel.

The ring was pink gold with a swirl of tiny beveled tear-drop diamonds. They sparkled and winked against their dark backdrop, and although Ericka's second emotion was rage, her first was a deep sigh of appreciation for the ring's loveliness.

She snapped shut the lid of the ring case and dug back into the pile of crumpled book reviews. Nothing else was there. She was perplexed, and this added to

146

her fury. Just what kind of game was Dexter playing here? Any minute she expected to hear a knock at her door, or a voice to emerge from her closet, "Smile! You're on Candid Camera!" She had an eerie sense of being followed, of not being alone. That feeling of intrusion made her even madder.

"Dexter, you bastard," she said out loud, just in case. "Don't you get it? After all this time? I hate you! You're a creep! Drop dead!"

There was no response to her outburst, though Blaze looked at her curiously from his place on top of the stereo. Ericka calmed herself and began to think. The answer was so simple. She'd take this ring and send it right back to Dexter, to the return address on the envelope.

She hoped she wouldn't have to move again. Ericka had lived in this guesthouse for almost seven years, and she'd never be able to get anything as good, even at twice the rent. Maybe she could still write "Return to Sender," even though she'd already opened it. "Opened By Mistake," she could print.

Satisfied with this solution, she reached for a pen and grabbed the jiffy bag, but this time as she picked it up, a small red envelope fell out of the open end.

Here we go, Ericka thought as she picked it up. Here comes the payoff. She sliced open the envelope that had her name on it and pulled out a one-page letter written in that same childlike hand. It was dated three days before.

Dear Ericka (and you are still very dear to me),

Give me a break, Dexter, she thought cynically.

I'm sure you thought you would never hear from me again. Please don't worry, I'm not going to bother you.

You already did!

I don't know if you'll believe this, but I look back on our relationship as the closest I have ever had with a woman of the opposite sex.

Poor Dexter. He's not even trying to be funny.

I don't know if you ever think about it at all, but I look back on that time with you as one of great hope and joy. Unfortunately, these are feelings I haven't experienced much since then. Although I have had some success in business, I haven't found anyone to share my life with.

And so, Ericka, I've decided to end my life. By the time you receive this letter, I will be just a memory.

I won't bore you with the details. I'm not writing to make you feel guilty, and I don't expect you to feel grief.

I want you to have this ring, which I've kept, because it was always meant for you to have. And I wanted you to know that I still remember you as one of the very best things in my life.

Love (always),

Dexter

Ericka set the letter on the bed, angrier than ever. Of all the stupid, manipulative, pushy things that Dexter had ever done, this was absolutely the worst. He was not going to get away with it.

Any minute her phone was going to ring, and on the other end of the line would be Dexter's goofy voice, saying, "Hi, did you get my letter?"

But another part of her felt sick with dread. She had never known Dexter to play a practical joke. She had never known him to be intentionally funny. If this was real . . .

Of course it's not real. People like Dexter Spivack didn't kill themselves. They just went on and on, inflicting their personalities on perfectly innocent people. Didn't they?

It occurred to Ericka that, in fact, she didn't know what kinds of people killed themselves. Sure, she'd thought of it herself from time to time, but only briefly, in passing moments of despair. Never seriously.

Ericka grabbed for the telephone and dialed long-distance information. She listened as a Brooklyn accent came over the line.

"What city please?"

"Manhattan. Do you have a listing for Spivack on . . ." she consulted the jiffy bag ". . . on 12th Street?" The accent recited the number, which she jotted on the back of the envelope.

She contemplated the dial again while she stared at the numbers. *Damn it, Dexter, if this is a hoax, I'll kill you.* If he answered, she could always hang up, she reasoned. But another part of her was praying as she gripped the receiver, *Dear God please let this be a hoax.*

She dialed, and listened to a faint, slow ring in an apartment on West 12th Street in New York City. It rang six times and then an answering machine clicked on. She heard Dexter's recorded voice say, "I can't come to the phone right now. Leave your message when you hear the beep."

Right, Dexter, really original. Relief made her flippant, but also renewed her sense of outrage. How dare he pull such a stupid trick on her!

Still, there was a nagging doubt. She tucked the ring box into a drawer and saved the jiffy bag, just in case she needed the return address. Then she went to bed, listening to the percussion of the rain as it beat against her metal awning. In the morning she couldn't remember her dreams.

A few days later she tried to call the New York number again. This time no machine picked up the call. The phone rang 10, 20, 30 times, tired and distant. It meant nothing, Ericka decided—he just left the machine off.

For a week she tried, every once in a while, but there was never an answer. In another week she got a tone and then a recorded message, announcing that the number she had dialed had been disconnected. He could have moved, she told herself.

Ericka was briefly tempted to call her mother up in San Francisco and tell her the story, but her ear could already imagine the distress and genuine sorrow

151

that would hollow her mother's voice. Something else, too, a low hum of reproach, or indictment. Or so Ericka feared.

She took to wearing the ring. It sparkled on her finger with a thousand lights, each one a penetrating beam, reflecting back her life: solitary, meager, her expectations worn thin as a butterfly's wing.

Sometimes people inquired about it. "Are you engaged?" they'd ask, eyeing the jewel with undisguised envy.

"I once was," she'd reply, and after a while she was no longer conscious that her response was anything less than the truth. "He died," she'd add, and the questioner would look embarrassed and mumble, "I'm sorry."

Ericka once tried to write a poem about it, but the words eluded her, flying about the room like sparks in the night sky, like the thousand lights cast by her engagement band.

TIDE POOLS

A Veri-tale by Briget Laskowski

*H*e *paused just outside the gates, as if to make sure of his freedom.* He lit a cigarette and waited. He almost expected to hear footsteps behind him or a voice reaching out to him. But the silence echoed around him and filled his head. Exhaling slowly, he walked towards the field opposite the gates and watched the cows ambling across the grass. One black and white cow raised her head and looked into his eyes. Her stare unsettled him. His hands began to shake, and he clasped them together hurriedly, then shoved them into his pockets. With one last glance at the red brick building behind him, he started down the path that led to the sea.

At night in his room he heard the sea, because the windows were open, and the sea filled his dreams. It brought back memories of waiting, listening, in the landing craft. The dreams had always been about tossing on the restless sea, then the smoke and the smell of fear, emanating from the other bodies huddled around him. The guns would pound in his head and he would wake up sweating. That's when he would hear the echoing pounding of the waves. They were waiting for him, mocking him with their constant presence.

As he had "improved," to use the doctor's word, the sea had become a background noise that ceased to frighten him. Now it was a constant companion and he wanted to see it once more. When he was a boy he had played with the sea, running along the sand, jumping in and out of the waves. Then he would charge into the ocean, and the waves would pluck him off his feet, duck him, and throw him onto the shore, where he would lie like some strange pink panting crab, before running back for more.

The path took him through the woods that from the windows of the hospital blocked his view of the sea. The woods were dark and sweet smelling. It was spring, and bluebells were spread like a patchwork quilt around the trees. He hadn't seen bluebells for six years. He stooped to pick one tender-headed stalk, but immediately, the blossom began to wilt, crumbling into a blue haze that smelled like his cigarette. He let the blossom fall to the earth and impatiently ground it into the dirt with his foot. His eyes fixed on the tiny blue mass on the ground. A small tic began jumping beside his eye and he reached up a shaking hand to quiet it.

He was amazed at the emotion flowing through him. This was the first time he had allowed himself to feel any emotion since he had taken refuge behind the thick black curtain of despair. Six years ago he had gratefully hidden himself behind the curtain and refused to write messages across his face. Since then he had drifted through endless days, tossed from therapy to therapy, doctor to doctor.

He remembered his mother coming to visit him. She was crying. He had held her in rigid arms and let her cry. When she had dried her eyes and blown her nose, she wanted to talk. He hadn't been able to understand her words, so he had watched her face. He remembered her eyes. Her puzzled look had stayed with him a long time, her moving lipsticked mouth, her grey hair, a little greyer each time she came. But her words made no sense, they were just noises in his head.

He shook himself impatiently—he didn't want to think of his mother—and continued to walk down the

path towards the sea. It was noisier now. The shushing
waves crashed against the rocky coast and he could
taste salt on his lips. Suddenly, he emerged from the
trees onto open land, where gorse bushes crouched,
their stubby roots grasping their piece of the earth, as
if daring the sea to rip it away.

He walked to the very edge of the cliff, where the
sea lay spread before him. The immensity caused him
to hesitate. He watched the moving grey bulk,
breathing, sighing, constantly seeking to envelop the
earth in its embrace; then reluctantly letting go,
moving away, sliding down the sand. Then, the
re-emergence of desire, and the headlong embrace of
the earth would begin again.

A small girl was sitting on a rocky outcrop,
crouched over a tide pool, watching the life within the
water. The cliff wasn't high, but it was rocky. He
searched until he found a well-worn path leading
down to the beach. He slid and scrambled down it,
taking with him a mixture of earth and stones. His feet
crunched on gravely sand. The smell of the sea was
strong: salt-laden wind, seaweed, rotting things, living
things, swimming and feeding on other living
things. It was the same smell that had invaded his
nostrils as a child. He walked the few yards that

separated him from the little girl who sat peering into the tide pool.

The child wasn't aware of his approach at first, then something alerted her, and from her perch on the rocks above him she watched him walk towards her. They regarded each other in silence until he felt impelled to speak.

"Hello," he said.

"Hello." She continued to stare at him. It made him nervous, and he reached for his cigarettes. It reminded him of the young doctor at the hospital, who had spent months trying to coax him out from behind that warm black curtain of nothingness and had at last brought him to the point where they would let him leave the hospital by himself and wander around. The only thing they had said before he left was, "Be back in time for tea." He knew that in the time-honored English tradition, tea would be precisely at four.

"Would you like to see?" the girl asked suddenly.

He nodded, stuffed the packet of cigarettes back into his pocket, and climbed up to sit beside her.

She moved away from him but pointed into the pool. "There's 'nemones. And see the little fish that play around them? Once, when I was little, I found a jellyfish. It was trapped, but there wasn't enough water and it died." She put her fingers into the tide pool and waved them around the sea anemone. The slender tentacles danced with her fingers. "If you touch them, ever-so-softly, they feel sticky."

He put his fingers into the water and touched the delicately pink sea-anemone. "It does feel sticky," he agreed. He glanced at her. She was studying him, especially his brown uniform.

"You're from The Nettles." He nodded, but she didn't need his confirmation. "My mother told me I shouldn't talk to you. She said some of you were . . . um . . ." She stopped, bit her lip, knowing instinctively that if she continued, she would hurt him in some way.

"I would like to talk to you. I haven't talked to a child in six years."

She stared at him, but her eyes were softer. "You haven't talked to anybody in all that time? I'm six." "Though I'll be seven in four months," she added as an afterthought.

"I've just been talking to grown-ups. There are no children at the hospital."

She nodded with her own understanding. "Children don't have things wrong inside their heads.

That's what my mum says. All the soldiers who live at The Nettles have things wrong inside their heads. I s'pose you do too."

"Have something wrong inside my head? Yes, I suppose you could put it like that."

"And are you all better now? You must be, or they wouldn't let you out all by yourself."

He wanted to reach out, touch her, tell her how much her simplicity warmed him, but he resisted, knowing it would frighten her. "Well, I'm much better. I'll be going home soon." His heart leapt inside his chest at hearing himself say those words, and he felt suddenly dizzy.

"That's good. Home's nice. I have a nice home. I have a mum and a daddy and a cat named Checkers."

"I have . . . had . . . a cat. Her name was . . . is . . . Lucy."

"Is she dead?"

"She's . . . I don't know. I forgot to ask my mother."

"You need to ask her. Cats are nice. Mine sleeps at the bottom of my bed, and when I turn over, she'll start to purr, and sometimes she'll come and rub her face against me."

"Lucy didn't sleep on my bed. She slept on the windowsill in my room. Sometimes I'd roll over and she'd open her eyes and look at me. I had the feeling she was watching over me." He smiled. It was the first time he had smiled in a long time and his face felt stiff, unused, somehow.

"Cats like to watch over people. They're smarter than people, and they like to remind themselves that they are." She glanced up, sniffed the air, and looked out at the sea. "Tide's turning," she said matter- of-factly.

He knew that once he could read the tides as she could. Just by the shift in the wind, the smell, he once knew if the tide was coming in or going out.

The breeze danced across the sand and blew at them playfully. It picked up stray brown tendrils of her hair and blew them around her face. She brushed them aside impatiently.

"There's bunkers just over those rocks. I s'pose you know all about them, being a soldier." She nodded her head to another group of rocks along the beach. "Did people really sit in those bunkers and shoot guns at people?"

He nodded, but his eyes had a far-away look.

"Did you do that?" It was almost an accusation.

He looked at her, startled at the intensity of her words. "No."

"But you did kill people. My Uncle Mike was in the war and he brought home a gun he took off a German soldier he killed. He was really pleased to have that gun."

"I didn't bring home anything." Nothing except memories—memories that wouldn't leave him alone at night.

"So, why are you at The Nettles?"

He didn't want to remember. He hadn't even told himself the whole story. He knew the facts, because they had told him, but he didn't want to think of himself doing the things they said he had done. His mind rebelled at the idea that he had killed . . . and killed . . . and killed again.

After the maelstrom that was the landing on the beach, his little band of warriors had hidden in a small village. It had once been a pretty village. Thatched roofs on white-washed cottages; a peaceful, bucolic place, suddenly thrust into the war to end all wars. Some of the thatch had been blown off the roofs, and gaping wounds appeared in the walls of the houses. The villagers had fled, taking little with them. They had left a cellarful of wine in the local cafe. That night he and his platoon got thoroughly drunk on that rough French wine.

They had taken and held the village. And as a reward they were ordered out, to begin an endless trek, with so many of their counterparts, across blasted, wasted land.

He had become a mindless killing machine. Sometimes his mind surfaced and was so appalled at what was going on around him that it hid itself and was blessedly numb again.

All he remembered of that particular day when he really lost it was that for three days they had been trying to take the little hill. Their squad had shrunk. Most of them were dead. The day before, he had held his best pal, Jimmy, in his arms for a long time. Jimmy had stared up into his eyes. He hadn't said anything, but his eyes had begged him to take the pain away. Eventually, mercifully, all the light had gone out of Jimmy's eyes, and there was no more pain.

Jimmy and he had started school together, two little nippers in short trousers. He remembered chasing Jimmy down the street and knocking him flat with one blow. (The air had gone out of Jimmy in just the same way it had when he died.) But Jimmy had got

164

up from the street and started to laugh and then knocked him flat in return. He had jumped on him, and they had rolled over and over in the road, punching each other, their laughter echoing off the grey walls around them.

Eventually, on that weary morning, in the middle of a field covered with crushed poppies, they had taken Jimmy away from him, and he had wrapped his arms around his knees and cried. He wasn't ashamed to cry; he had seen a lot of other men do it now. There was nothing manly or brave in war, and he had no sacred or secret emotions to be ashamed of.

The next day, it had rained. They crouched in the mud, still waiting to take the hill. Dawn broke with smeary weariness. The sergeant had gathered them in a huddle around him and ordered them to take the little hill. He had done his best to rally them, trying to instill stiff-upper-lips and all-for-oneness.

He was remembering now. It wasn't a story he had heard them tell him over and over again at the hospital. It was a real memory. He had reached out his hand, picked up Jimmy's rifle, and run towards the top of the hill. He was firing crazily, randomly, at anything that moved. But there were no answering shots. The enemy had silently retreated during the night.

It had all been for nothing. Nothing. Jimmy and all the others had died for nothing.

At first, in his anger, he had run around the hill, shouting and swearing at the enemy, demanding that they come back and be killed. He was furious with them for denying him his revenge. Then he collapsed in a heap and started to laugh, and laugh . . . and laugh. He hadn't been able to stop. The medics had come and dragged him away, and he continued to laugh. He laughed so much that tears streamed down his face and he wet his trousers. It was the laughing that had brought him home, to The Nettles.

"You're not going to tell me, are you?" The child moved, and brushed his hand with her own, breaking into his thoughts.

He was back on the beach, the sea moving softly, creeping towards them. He looked down into the accusing eyes of the child.

"What did you want to know?" He put his hand to his head. "I'm sorry . . . "

"Did you kill anyone?"

"Yes."

"Was it all right?"

"No."

"My Daddy said that war is not good. He said that sometimes it's something grown-ups have to do, but that it's not . . ." she hesitated ". . . not nice."

"It's terrible."

She stretched out her fingers and wrapped them around his hand. They were warm, sun-browned fingers and they reached all the way to his heart. He smiled at her.

"Does your head hurt?"

"No, my head feels much better. It feels light and much happier."

"The sea makes people feel like that. When I feel sad, I come down to the sea and it makes me laugh. Sometimes I find things, interesting things."

"I found something today," he said.

"What?"

"You."

"Oh, I don't mean people. I mean interesting things. Once I found a piece of pretty red glass with smooth edges all around. I thought it was a jewel, but my mum said it was just glass. I kept it though. I still have it."

"What else have you found?"

"Lots of things. All kinds of shells and pretty rocks. Once I found a dead sea-gull. I told my daddy, and he came down and buried it. I made a cross out of lollipop sticks."

"That's sad."

"My mum told me that he was in heaven, with Jesus."

He remembered his own mother, telling him the same thing when their old dog had died. He must have been about ten years old, and her simple way of explaining that Raffles had gone to heaven had comforted him. He could picture Raffles, panting after a tall, shining figure who was striding through white clouds.

Suddenly, he realized that he was happy. He had remembered his mother doing something other than visiting him in the hospital. It was as if floodgates had opened and he was immersed in memories. He thought of his mother, singing as she washed the dishes in their kitchen, always hymns on Sunday; his dad, sleeping in his chair after the Sunday roast; his brother, Joe, all nervous on his wedding day. And . . . and he remembered Marie Clare, sitting in front of the Christmas tree, shaking her presents.

"I want to open one . . . just one . . . please, please," she would say. The memories invaded his heart and his mind, crowding each other, jostling together in their haste to be seen. He was awash in warmth and happiness.

"What's funny?"

He realized that he had been smiling—more than smiling—grinning from ear to ear.

"I was remembering . . . happy things. Christmas and stuff."

"It's a long time to wait for Christmas." She sighed.

"I had a little sister," he began softly. "She loved Christmas."

"So do I. Is she dead?"

"She was killed in the war."

Her eyes grew round. "How?"

It was just a stray bomb. Someone dumping off the last of their load. It landed on my house . . . and she died." Funny, he hadn't thought about her at all . . . not since he got that letter from his mother, telling him that she was dead.

"Was she pretty?"

"I hadn't thought about it. . . . Yes, I suppose she was."

"Did she have blue eyes, like yours?"

"Yes. Big blue eyes."

She sighed. "Then she was pretty. You'll miss her for a long time."

"Always."

"I don't have any brothers or sisters. I miss not having anyone to talk to, but sometimes it's nice to be alone. I think a lot."

"I can tell you do."

"I'm a very"—she drew herself up—"a very self-reliant person." She enunciated the words very carefully. "But I have to go home now." She stood up and began to climb down from her perch among the rocks. He clambered awkwardly after her.

"Let me walk with you across the beach."

"Why?" She turned and placed her hands on her hips and glared at him. He was startled at her abrupt change of mood.

"Because I want to."

"Oh, well, I s'pose that's all right. But I'm not a little baby. I come down here by myself all the time."

170

"I would like to walk with you." She nodded at him, then slipped her hand into his. A strange thrill, like an electric charge, passed through him. He looked down at her and grinned. His eyes crinkled.

"You have nice eyes," she said. "Pretty blue eyes, like my cousin, Alice. I wish I had pretty blue eyes. I just have old brown ones. Like mud."

"I like brown eyes."

"I'd like to have orange eyes, like my cat. If I can't have blue, I'll have orange."

"You look nice with brown eyes. I like them much better than any old orange eyes."

She stopped and looked at him closely. "You're teasing."

"Yes."

They stood at the bottom of the cliff. She jumped up onto a rock and turned to look at him as she spoke.

"Are you going back to the hospital now?"

"No. I think I'll stay here for a while. Do some thinking. By the way what is your name? I'd like to remember you, I could do that better if I knew your name."

171

"Genevieve. Yuck. But most people call me Genny . . . with a 'G'. What was your sister's name?"

"Marie Clare."

"Gosh, what a pretty name. Much nicer than mine. Do you think she would mind if I called myself that . . . sometimes. When I come to the beach, I'll pretend my name is Marie Clare, and I'll think about you, too. 'Though I won't tell my mother about you. She'd be angry 'cause I talked to you."

"Goodbye, Genny-with-a-G. I'm glad I met you this afternoon, and I don't think Marie Clare would mind if you used her name."

"Did you like the 'nemones? Go back and look at the 'nemones. They're very pretty. And there's some orange ones in the pools down the beach." She pointed and then turned to climb up the cliff on her hands and knees. When she reached the top, she turned and waved. "Bye," she called.

He waved back and then she was gone. He turned back to the beach and the sea. The waves were creeping closer, a stealthy recapturing of the sand. If he hurried, he could look at Genny's 'nemones once more before the water covered them.

He crossed back to the rocky outcrop and climbed up to sit in the sun and watch the lazy anemones as they carved the water with their sticky tentacles. He lit a cigarette, leaned back, and closed his eyes.

The next low tide, after the sea had replenished the pool, the anemones would still be there, moving lazily when stirred by inquisitive fingers; and little fish would be swimming amongst them. The bunkers would still be squatting with empty eyes gazing out at the sea, endlessly watching for an enemy that would never come.

He lit another cigarette and decided he would walk along the beach and look at the bunkers. He would look at them, and he would not see or hear the guns. But he would remember. Part of him would always be back there, hearing the guns, smelling the smoke, holding dead Jimmy in his arms. But now he could remember the good times, too. The tide had turned.

He tossed his cigarette into the air and watched the small blazing spark, that hissed softly as it hit the water. He smiled to himself and began to run along the beach, jumping in and out of the playful waves.

A LYCURGUS CHRISTMAS CANTATA

A Veri-tale by Robert Dodge

Over at the school the Millers have spent most of the week working on the annual Christmas cantata. Every year the cantata shows Mary and Joseph arriving in Bethlehem, and, of course, there is no room in the inns.

Jack always worries because he has to find nine male soloists, which is always three more than he thinks he has, but that's how many the cantata calls for. This year Alice has her share pretty well under control. She has managed to find plenty of female soloists, and she knows that most of them will hit the right notes and sing the right words. But she wants to get them as close to perfect as she can, so she has them and the choruses working every possible minute.

Jack and Alice Miller have lived in Lycurgus for almost thirty years. Both of them teach music at the school. Jack gives instrumental lessons and directs the band, the male chorus, and the orchestra. Alice teaches elementary music and directs the girls' chorus, the mixed chorus, and the junior band. Jack has the choir at the Presbyterian Church and Alice has the choir at the Episcopal. They get paid for their church work, but each of them gives the money back to the church. They don't tell anyone.

Right now, they're each more worried about the cantata than anything else. The cantata is, after all, one of the two biggest yearly events in Lycurgus. It ranks right up there with the Fourth of July celebration.

Jack often talks about changing the Christmas program. "We could put on the cantata every three or four years and have choral music in the auditorium or even go caroling around the village the other years." But he knows it wouldn't work. Some of the people in the town just wouldn't feel it was really Christmas unless they could see the Holy Family turned away from the innkeepers' doors. They like to see the Three Wise Men and the shepherds and the angels. Somehow it brings back the real meaning of Christmas, some of them say.

Wally Decker, Alice's brother, says if he wants to see a bunch of kids in bathrobes, he can stand in his own hallway during the morning rush on the bathroom. If he wants to be reminded of the real meaning of Christmas, he can go to church.

When they hear this, Jack and Alice smile. They know Wally will be there at the cantata. Four of his kids are in it. And one of them has a solo.

Nearly every parent in Lycurgus will go to the cantata. Jack and Alice have shared this knowledge for thirty years, and if they have one secret from the rest of Lycurgus, it is simply this: Lots of kids who don't really sing all that well become part of the chorus. "It helps to build the audience," Alice says. And Jack knows she's right. Jack and Alice consider it a bonus that once in a while a chorus member develops into a good singer.

Yes, Wally will come. He will watch and listen, as Young Wally sings his short solo. And Wally will be satisfied. Jack wonders if anyone else will feel satisfied with that solo.

Young Wally was the last soloist chosen for the cantata. He plays the part of the third innkeeper, and Jack thinks Bethlehem had one inn too many. He thought about cutting an inn out of the script, but everyone in Lycurgus has seen the cantata so many times, it's too late to change it. They like it exactly the way it is. So Jack had to cast a third innkeeper, and it was either Young Wally or nobody. Jack went with Young Wally.

In some ways Young Wally was a good choice. He is a hard worker, and he's absolutely delighted to have his own solo. There's one high note he can't hit, but the composer provided an alternate for that note, and Wally hits the alternate fairly consistently. Unfortunately, Jack has a much bigger concern than whether Wally will hit the note.

He's worried about Wally's pronunciation. Not that it's much different from that of most of the kids in Lycurgus. Wally slurs, and, sometimes he makes his short *e's* sound like short *i's,* and, sometimes his final *d's* sound like *t's.* And that's a problem, because the third innkeeper has to tell the Holy Family to go sleep in the cowshed.

Then there's the Harrison boy. At the auditions, which Jack held near the end of October, the Harrison boy sang a fine tenor. Jack cast him as one of the kings. Now his voice is changing faster than any voice Jack has ever known. Jack has already rearranged the music twice and he's afraid he'll have to do it a third time. The Harrisons have no idea what a job it is to rearrange a work of music, but even if they did, Jack knows there's nothing they could do about Charles's voice. At rehearsal Charles was singing about myrrh, and his voice cracked right in the middle of "its bitter perfume." They went back, he sang it again, and that time it was beautiful. Jack knows that someday Charles will become a fine baritone or even a bass. He just wonders when.

Sometimes Jack envies Alice. Girls' voices don't change. But Alice is going to have problems of her own pretty soon. Susan Flanders thinks she may be pregnant. "How could this have happened?" she asks herself.

She knows how it could have happened; what she's wondering is if she should tell anyone. She wonders if she'll show by the time of the cantata. She wonders if it won't be sacrilegious to play the Virgin Mary while she's pregnant. She thinks that tomorrow she'll tell Mrs. Miller that she can't be in the cantata. She probably won't tell her why. She

179

should, though, because Alice knows about such things.

Alice would tell her that she wouldn't be the first—and she wouldn't. Since Alice started to teach music in Lycurgus, at least two Virgins have played the part while they were pregnant. Susan, of course, doesn't know that. Alice would tell her that although Mary got there another way, she was pregnant, too. Maybe it's appropriate to be with child. But Susan is an old-fashioned girl. She's ashamed. She won't tell.

It was just that one time, and she was out with the best-looking boy in the class ahead of hers. He'd told her all of his dreams and plans and she'd told him all of hers, and they just sort of fell together, even though each of them had just finished saying that one of their dreams was to be a virgin when they got married.

The next day they'd both been too ashamed to look at one another, but the boy—Young Wally, as a matter of fact—came looking for her after school. Soon they were walking together. They didn't say much until they arrived at one of Susan's favorite places, the hill behind her house, where ten years ago, as a 4-H project, her older brother had planted seven hundred seedling spruce trees. This year, for the first time, they would cut one down for Christmas.

Susan found a dry spot beneath one of the trees and made Wally sit four feet away beneath another one. Wally started talking. He told her they had to forget about last night, that he still loved her and wanted to go out with her, but from now on they "had to be good." Wally couldn't believe he'd said that. He knew how stupid he sounded. But he must have found just the right words. Susan felt so relieved she could have kissed him right there, but she didn't. She knew where that could lead.

Tomorrow will be a rehearsal of the entire cast. At that dress rehearsal Young Wally will sing "cowshed" very distinctly; Susan will radiate the good health and joy of a young woman who has just found out she's not pregnant; Charles's voice will crack only once. There will still be a few rough spots, but they will make a tape of the dress rehearsal, and there will be a week yet to get the last bugs out.

After the rehearsal Jack and Alice will take the tape home, and that night they will go into their bedroom and lie in bed as they listen to it. For a few moments they will rest together in the beauty of the music, because it is music that they love, and because they are teachers, and like any teachers, they are most happy when they are giving away that which they

181

most love. For thirty years they have given Lycurgus the gift of music. No one ever said it would be easy.

Then they will rewind the tape and listen again, this time more critically, to the music of their newest cantata. They will hear Charles's voice break once. Alice will say it won't break on the day of the performance, and Jack will know she means that even if it does break, it will be all right. They will hear the sweet tones coming from Susan's mouth, and Alice will think that something was wrong with her, but she's worked it out now, and Alice will smile. Then that sweet, sweet music will wash over them, and they will both fall asleep. In the morning they'll get back to work.

BIOGRAPHICAL SKETCHES

a brief introduction to the authors and the illustrators
of *VeriTales: Ring of Truth*

Judy Bell Carlton, parent, sixth grade teacher, and free-lance writer, focuses her life on "trying to make a difference in the world." Her non-fiction writing reflects that focus: "An Ex-nun's Life in the Convent," for the SOCIAL ISSUES RESOURCES SERIES; "Yoga and Meditation in the Classroom," for HOLISTIC EDUCATION; and numerous articles for the Blood Center of Southeast Wisconsin and the National Bone Marrow Registry. That same universal concern for mankind is evident in her portrayal of "Laundry Larry," who brings us "glimpses of our own self-limitations, frustration, hope, and perhaps the courage to do what we believe is right."

Robert Dodge, professor of English at the University of Nevada, Las Vegas, and specialist in early American literature, comes from a long line of oral storytellers, carrying on the tradition of his father, grandfather, and great-grandfather. Like "Cantata," many of his published stories began as his expression of that long oral tradition, evolving into the written form in such periodicals as THE SNOWY EGRET, THE LAS VEGAN CITY MAGAZINE, and THE MINNESOTA REVIEW OF BASEBALL. Much of the heritage of small town Americana is communicated in his stories of "Lycurgus"; a fictional town very similar to Cincinnatus, New York, where Bob grew up, and in tribute to whose teachers, including his own parents, "A Lycurgus Christmas Cantata" was written.

Janet Howey's past professional experience includes work as diverse as owning her own street vending falafel business and working as a personnel manager. She has also been a rape victim advocate, land use planner, masseuse, and business manager for a law firm. She currently works as administrator in an AIDS hospice and has an active meditation practice. Janet is fond of saying that nothing she has ever done is related to anything else she has ever done. She suspects, however, that that is not true, and she uses her writing to explore and strengthen the threads of commonality in her life. Her work has recently appeared in ART AND UNDERSTANDING, TRICYCLE, and JAMA.

Briget Laskowski brings to her writing the flavor of her international heritage. Born in England, she lived for several years in the Bahamas, where she married an American from Detroit. They settled finally in Arkansas, where she is pursuing a Master's Degree in expository writing, while working as Assistant Director of the Writing Center at the University of Arkansas at Little Rock. "Tide Pools" grew out of a brief encounter with a soldier which she had as a child on a beach in England. "My mother had warned me about this, but I was a stubborn child and did talk to him." Remembering the sadness in the soldier's eyes, many years later she wrote this story "so that he might be happy again."

William Luvaas "arrived" on the literary scene with the publication of his novel, THE SEDUCTIONS OF NATALIE BACH.

One of those rare first novels taken "over the transom" by a major publishing house, it was published by Little, Brown and described by NEWSDAY as "one of the best works of fiction about the 60's." That work was followed by two other novels, wide publication of his stories, and being named 1986 co-winner of FICTION NETWORK'S National Fiction Competition. Luvaas has received writing fellowships from The Edward Albee Foundation and the Ludwig Vogelstein Foundation, and has been Fiction Coordinator for Poets in Public Service in New York. He currently teaches writing at the University of California, San Diego, and San Diego State University.

David Shapiro, freelance writer, psychologist, master electrician, and practitioner of Structural Integration, describes himself as "humanist, libertarian, and a devout agnostic, with a grave distrust of institutions and belief systems which encourage people to say, 'I'm doing this not because I want to but because he/she/it says it's right.' I respect the tough, and not the mean; the brave, and not the careless; the competent, and not the greedy; the percipient, and not the neurotically self-directed; the straight-forward, and not the insensitive."

Beverly Sheresh, a New Englander transplanted in Southern California, brings to her writing the artistry of a thoroughly artistic family. "A Secret Place" reflects the author's heritage, rich in music, painting, and literature.

Her mother had an orchestra of her own; her grandfather was known as a master of the trombone and the violin and a rousing square dance fiddler; her cousin played saxophone with Les Brown; but Beverly's "favorites" are Mozart, Saint-Saens, Bach, Beethoven. Her husband, Gene, is also a published writer. Beverly's work has been published in YANKEE, KALEIDOSCOPE, ST. ANTHONY'S MESSENGER, MIRACULOUS MEDAL, MIDNIGHT ZOO, ECHOES MAGAZINE, DOWN EAST, and SENIOR MAGAZINE. She is currently working on a novel titled THE SPIRIT WHO WAITS.

Ron Suppa describes himself as "a South Philly boy with nebulous ties to Hollywood." A former entertainment lawyer, he has written and produced a number of feature motion pictures. Recently, Ron has co-written the historical novel, LORD BYRON'S DAUGHTER, and was the recipient of the 1991 Outstanding Teacher Award for his screen-writing classes at UCLA Extension. An acknowledged Anglophile, Ron's writing seminars in London were the subject of a recent BBC special program.

John Vorhaus is a bit of a maverick. He describes his approach to life as, "First get the job, then figure out how to do it"; an approach perhaps stemming from a time when "hard pressed for cash, I got myself hired as a stilt-walker—and then learned how to walk on stilts." John's teaching and writing credits include episodes of the television shows, THE WONDER YEARS, MARRIED . . . WITH

CHILDREN, and HEAD OF THE CLASS. He has also written for such disparate publications as SPY MAGAZINE and SPORTS ILLUSTRATED. He teaches screenwriting, comedy, and creativity, and lectures regularly at writing conferences nationwide. As the reader of "Josie" will quickly recognize, John's off-beat world-view is overlaid on a profound philosophical base, well expressed in the words, "This I believe above all other things: A man shall find goodness if goodness he brings."

Sharlie West is a widow and mother of three daughters. A free-lance writer and psychic counselor, she specializes in intuitive readings and distance healing. In her veri-tale, "Requiem," the main character, suffering from the traumatic death of a child and the inability of the parents to adjust, "has walled herself off from humanity, yet wants desperately to break through." Drawing on her personal and professional understandings, Sharlie portrays the "intuitive love of another, allowing that character to transcend the state of numbness and slowly, painfully, rejoin the living."

Terry Wolverton is a multi-talented human being. Since 1976 she has lived in Los Angeles, where she has been active in the feminist, gay and lesbian, and art communities. Her work of fiction, poetry, essays, and drama has been published in periodicals internationally and has been widely anthologized. Terry has received six

California Arts Council Artist-in-Residence grants in literature. She is currently at work on her first novel, THE LABRYS REUNION. In addition to writing, Terry has toured North America as a performance artist and has produced audio and video art, as well as installations. She is the former Executive Director of the widely respected Woman's Building, a public center for women's culture in Los Angeles.

Gail Tomura is a nationally exhibited multi-media artist. For the interior illustrations of *VeriTales, Ring of Truth,* she has chosen the medium of watercolors and the theme of the human hand. Like all of Gail's work, her illustrations carry the viewer beyond the medium, stimulating the pursuit of one's own thoughts, and thus, one's own path of spiritual growth.

We acknowledge and appreciate the work of **Roger Hillman,** of Portland, Oregon, in both cover design and production supervision; the cover photography by **Russ Illig**, also of Portland; and the printing expertise—and commitment to the use of recycled paper—of **Thomson-Shore, Inc.** The technical expertise of each of these skilled professionals has been invaluable in the production of this first *VeriTales* anthology.

To **Helen Wirth**, editor, goes credit for the editorial and the spiritual eye which has both identified and enhanced the magic that lies within this collection of veri-tales.

The Magic of *VeriTales* Continues...

This source of wonder and personal triumph has not ended just because you have turned the last page. This is only the beginning of VeriTales.

Ring of Truth is the first in an on-going series of VeriTales anthologies. *VeriTales: Note of Hope* continues where *VeriTales: Ring of Truth* leaves off.

On the pages that follow, you will find the Expanded Table of Contents for *VeriTales: Note of Hope.* Take a moment to read these brief notes about the upcoming veri-tales. Let the magic continue in your life. Place your advance order today.

TABLE OF CONTENTS

VeriTales: Note of Hope

Available September, 1993

VeriTales: Note of Hope will be available through select bookstores and direct from the publisher, Fall Creek Press.

To order direct, call:

Toll-free 1-800-964-1905

Monday through Thursday, 9:00-5:00 PST. Please have your VISA or Mastercard ready.

Or mail your order, including the following information:

Name and shipping address (printed clearly)

Daytime telephone number

Name of book(s) and how many of each

VeriTales: Note of Hope @ $14.95
VeriTales: Ring of Truth @ $14.95

Enclose $2.00 per book shipping within U.S.
(On orders of 3 books or more, shipping/handling within the United States is FREE.)

Mail advance orders to:

Fall Creek Press
P.O. Box 1127
Fall Creek, OR 97438